Meredith Webber lives on the sunny Gold Coast in Queensland, Australia, but takes regular trips west into the Outback, fossicking for gold or opal. These breaks in the beautiful and sometimes cruel red earth country provide her with an escape from the writing desk and a chance for her mind to roam free—not to mention getting some much-needed exercise. They also supply the kernels of so many stories that it's hard for her to stop writing!

A WIFE FOR THE SURGEON SHEIKH

MEREDITH WEBBER

MILLS & BOON

Published in Great Britain 2019
by Mills & Boon, an imprint of HarperCollins*Publishers*
1 London Bridge Street, London, SE1 9GF

© 2019 Meredith Webber

ISBN: 978-0-263-07954-8

MIX
Paper from
responsible sources
FSC™ C007454

This book is produced from independently certified FSC™ paper
to ensure responsible forest management.
For more information visit www.harpercollins.co.uk/green.

Printed and bound in Great Britain
by CPI Group (UK) Ltd, Croydon, CR0 4YY

CHAPTER ONE

LAUREN SUPPOSED SHE had known there'd be an executive director of finance and logistics—after all, someone would have to look after the money side of the hospital—but in the nearly two years she'd worked here she'd never heard of Mr Marshall, to whose office she had been summoned at the end of her shift.

Was there something wrong with her superannuation? No, she was sure chief executives had more important things to do than worry about very minor employees' superannuation.

So, what could he possibly want?

Unanswerable questions kept worry at bay as the elevator rose to the rarefied air of the sixth floor, but walking down the corridor in search of Room 279 she found panic building…

A beautifully dressed secretary—or perhaps a personal assistant—looked her up and down, and offered a disdainful eyebrow lift at the sight of her dishevelled end-of-shift clothes, which were probably bloodstained somewhere an apron didn't cover, before ushering her through a door into the inner sanctum.

'Sister Macpherson,' the woman announced, and Lauren stepped forward, wondering which of the two men was Mr Marshall. Surely not the one in the grey silk suit that hung on him with such precision he could have been a model in a very expensive tailor's shop.

A very good-looking model, from what she could see, as he stood with the light behind him. Although his shoulders were probably wider than the norm so the suit had, undoubtedly, been tailor-made.

But Silk Suit remained by the window, studying her, she was sure, from beneath heavy eyelids.

Hawk's eyes…

Hooded…

Scanning for prey?

She felt a shiver of apprehension, and a slight stirring of something she couldn't quite place, and definitely didn't want to think about…

'I'm Ted Marshall,' the other man said, interrupting her fantasy and stepping forward. He held out his hand towards Lauren and positively radiated goodwill. 'Please, come in and sit down. Sheikh Madani has something he wishes to discuss with you, and as he's come a long way to see our new children's wing, the very least I can do is offer him the hospitality of my room.'

Twit!

But the name he'd mentioned—it couldn't be… It was impossible.

Though of course it had to be, and as a feeling of inevitability all but swamped her, Lauren told herself she was *not* afraid.

Well, not much…

Practically falling over himself to please Silk Suit, Ted Marshall waved the other visitor forward, though Lauren hadn't sat down, flight-or-fight instinct telling her she'd be better off on her feet.

'Sheikh Madani, this is Sister Macpherson. Now, I'll leave the two of you to discuss your business.'

Leave her here with Madani?

No way!

She knew the name Madani only too well. Knew it and hated it with a passion. Hadn't it been a Madani who had stolen her sister?

'You can't do that!' she said to the departing Mr Marshall. 'You can't get me up here and leave me in a room with a total stranger because he praised your new hospital! That's irresponsible and unethical and probably illegal!'

She knew her cheeks were probably scarlet and her hair was probably standing on end, and forget being afraid—terror had prompted her outburst. Not for herself, but for Nim.

Silk Suit watched from the window, his eyes, lids lifted now, focussed in her direction.

And if that was a smirk twitching at his lips, she'd kill him.

Or get Joe to kill him.

'You need fear no danger from me,' the man said, his voice as smooth as the sleek clothes he wore, the accompanying smile as friendly as a shark's.

'There, you see,' Ted Marshall said, edging closer to the door. 'The sheikh has business with the hospital then mentioned wanting to see you. Apparently, there's a family matter he wishes to discuss with you, and I'm sure it would be to your advantage to listen to him.'

And on that note he scuttled out of the door.

Lauren remained where she was, paralysed by the knowledge that this man might well have been behind the murder of her sister and parents.

And if not him, surely one of his relations…

But there was no way she could reveal the panic in her heart or the clutch of icy fingers gripping her stomach.

She took a deep breath, and aimed for being cool.

'You have business with me?'

Cool *and* polite.

'I think you know I do.'

His deep, treacly voice rasped against her skin and sent shivers down her spine, but Lily had been taken in by a treacly voice and silk suits—by money, and jewellery, and private planes that swept her from one holiday playground to the next.

Beautiful, vibrant, fun-loving Lily…

And look how that had ended.

'Oh?' Lauren managed, dragging herself out of the past, and ignoring the catch in her own breathing as he moved closer.

'The boy! You have the boy!'

It wasn't a question, but how much did he actually know?

Not where she lived or he'd have come to the house— possibly even kidnapped Nim—though that would have happened over Joe's dead body.

'What boy?' she asked, stalling.

He waved away her pretence, eyes like obsidian boring into hers.

'He needs to be taken home.' His voice was glacial now. 'He needs to know the country he will one day rule.'

'And just who are you to be making these demands?'

The man drew himself up to an impressive height and seemed to summon a sense of power from the ether.

'I am Abdul-Malik Madani, I am called Malik, and my name means Protector of the King.'

Refusing to be intimidated, Lauren straightened, and although five feet five wasn't a very impressive height, she made the most of it with a tilt of her chin and a glare in her eyes.

'Well, if Nim's father was the former heir, then you didn't do too good a job of it!'

She heard his reaction—a quick snatch of breath—and saw it in the stricken look on his face, the sudden bowing of his head to hide his emotion.

She watched his chest expand as he breathed deeply,

and knew the depth of his pain when he spoke again, voice strained with grief.

'You are right,' he said. 'I could not save my brother, but it is his son that I must protect now—protect at all costs, even with my life.'

That was a bit melodramatic, but hadn't all her admittedly brief contact with the Madanis been overly melodramatic?

She closed her eyes, remembering, shuddering, aware of this man's presence in every cell of her being, trying to focus on what he was saying.

He was either a consummate actor or genuine, but did she really want to find out which?

She moved towards the door, intending to keep walking until she was well away from this man. Somewhere quiet where she *could* think quietly and halt the panic.

But in two strides he had overtaken her so he now stood directly in front of her—less than a foot away—towering over her with some kind of inner presence that made her feel more queasy than afraid.

Strange, unsettled butterflies rioted in her stomach, zapping their disquiet along her nerves. Up close, the man's face was beautiful—not in a pretty-boy way but with hard carved features: a thin straight nose separating those deep-set eyes; high ridges of cheekbones; and lips full enough for his mouth to scream sensual but not too full—not fleshy, just there, unsmiling...

'The child's name is Nimr!'

The words were like a slap.

So much for her thinking she'd scored a point on him earlier.

'We call him Nim,' she retorted. 'Easier than trying to roll that unfamiliar "r" at the end. But, yes, it's spelled Nimr on official documents.'

'And yet you asked what boy?'

Sarcasm iced the words and Lauren felt them cut into her skin—saying Nim's name had brought back the fear. Just because this man said he'd give his life for Nim, what proof was that?

For all Lauren knew, he could have been behind his brother's death.

As soon as she thought it, she knew she shouldn't have gone there—memories threatened to swamp her again and right now she needed to be strong.

As for his assumption that Nim would want to be King of the godforsaken country this man was talking about—well, that was for the future, *and* for Nim himself to decide!

'Nim was left in my care and that's where he stays,' Lauren said, not adding Lily's almost hysterical warning of deadly danger. Of people—Tariq's family members even—trying to track her down to kill her and her son. And Lauren, for her sins, had dismissed it all, sure Lily had been exaggerating—blaming her state on a hormone-fuelled fantasy.

That was until the accident, and then when Nim had been taken…

Don't go there, she told her frantic thoughts.

'And now I need to leave,' she said, taking a side step, hoping to get behind him to the door—

Which proved hopeless.

She tried a glare, one that usually sent overexcited adolescents straight back to their beds, but felt it bounce off him.

'Perhaps we should begin again, discuss this in more congenial surroundings. As Mr Marshall said, I had some business with the hospital, and thought you might feel more at ease meeting me here with other people's knowledge of the meeting. But there are other places…'

He touched her, oh, so lightly on the shoulder as he

spoke, and fire spread through her body, confirming the danger she'd felt in this man from the beginning.

Was this how Lily had felt when she'd first met Tariq?

'There's nothing to discuss,' she told him, forcing her voice to stay firm. 'Nim is my child, properly adopted. He stays here!'

'With security lights all around your house, and alarms hard-wired back to the police station, and a guard to follow him wherever he goes?'

Panic swelled in Lauren.

He *did* know where she lived! And *how* they lived! The only thing he didn't know was her constant fear...

But there was no way this man was going to get her child!

'He's not a guard, he's a nanny,' she snapped. 'Most working mothers have them!'

'Six-two male? SAS-trained? Do most Australian working mothers have such a nanny?'

She stepped back, aware of giving ground, but she couldn't yell at him successfully when she was so close. Something about the man flustered her and she was pretty sure it wasn't fear...

She took another deep breath.

'I lost my entire family in that accident—everyone but Nim—and no one can tell me how or why it happened, or, worse, who the target was. I don't know whether it was my sister and our parents, or your brother.'

'There was a doubt about the intended victim?' he demanded, his voice sharp with tension as he broke into her explanation.

Closing her eyes briefly to regain a little composure, Lauren explained.

'My father had many business interests in the west,

from mining to pastoral holdings and beyond. The police thought…'

She couldn't go on, remembering the horror of those days when grief had been overwhelming her and policemen had been constantly asking questions—

'Tell me.'

His voice was gentle now, not a plea exactly but with enough emotion in it that she understood he needed to know.

'It was only when Nim was snatched they turned their attention to your brother.'

'Someone took the child?'

His eyes blazed with anger now, but the memories were pressing down on her and she had to get the story told before she broke down from the remembered terror.

'A police family liaison officer was staying with me. The detectives were there one morning with so many questions, their voices unsettled Nim. He was only tiny. So I took him out for a walk in his pram, and someone hit me on the head and ran off with him.'

She tried to quell the memories of her pain and fear. She had thought that not only had she lost her parents and Lily but the baby as well—the baby she'd promised Lily she'd protect.

Had he read it in her eyes that he steered her back into a chair.

'Sit, take deep breaths! They found the child?'

He asked the question in the same calm voice he'd used to make her sit.

She nodded.

'At the airport, dressed all in pink, travelling on a passport as Lucy someone, two parents travelling with her. It was luck, nothing more, that they found Nim—another twenty minutes and they'd have boarded, the plane doors would have shut.'

'And the couple?

Lauren looked up at the man hovering impatiently in front of her.

'They admitted to being paid to kidnap the child and take him to the United States, where he could be sold to adoptive parents in some quasi-criminal deal. But they denied all knowledge of the accident. Further police investigations couldn't prove they'd been involved.'

She read confusion in his eyes and understood it, for those few months of her life still seemed unreal to her.

But this man needed answers, so she picked up where she'd left off earlier.

'So, yes, I have security to protect my child, but none of it intrudes on his having a normal childhood. That is one thing I work very hard to ensure.'

Lauren paused, needing to catch her breath, needing to see his face—his expression—as she finalised this business.

'So, really, there's nothing else to discuss. I'm guessing you spent a considerable amount of money to track me down, but Nim is mine now—a little Australian boy with a future here, not in his father's country. So I'll be getting home to my son.'

'Son? You *have* adopted him?'

She'd been expecting more objections to her leaving, not this shocked disbelief.

'Lily left him with me that night, telling me to take great care of him—telling me again of threats. To do that when she was…' Lauren made a huge effort to pull herself together '…gone, he had to be legally mine, so of course I've adopted him.'

She looked directly into his eyes this time—into darkness that held no light or shadows, and about as much humanity and understanding as a statue's blank gaze.

Malik was only too aware he'd made a mess of this. First the fawning executive, setting up the meeting with this woman as if he was conferring a great honour on her.

And then underestimating the stubborn female who'd had the guts to adopt his nephew. There might not be much of her, and most of what he could see was tired and grubby, but despite the dark shadows beneath her large grey eyes, and the fear, which had been an almost palpable thing in the room, she'd stood up to him.

Though with what she'd been through he could understand that fear...

Coming here, he'd thought she'd be willing to hand the boy over to him—perhaps with due recompense—but every word he'd heard held the cadences of her love for Nimr.

Had he been judging her by her sister, that he'd thought this way? One look at her had dispelled any physical resemblance, and he doubted Lily would have stood up to him the way Lauren had, or taken the extreme measures he now knew of, to keep his nephew safe.

No, Lily had been beautiful, captivating, and could charm birds from a tree, but how much more attractive was the courage and quiet determination of this sister?

Something he hadn't felt for a long time stirred inside him, something he'd have to think about later, because his business was far from finished.

As far as she was concerned, Nimr was her child and she'd probably have killed him if he'd mentioned recompense.

He looked down at her, close now as she tried once more to get out the door, and he was almost sure he detected a tremble in her body, and definitely saw fear behind the defiance in her eyes.

He touched her gently on the shoulder—felt the tremors running through her and the coldness of her skin and knew he hadn't imagined the fear, knew he'd caused it, and that wounded him.

'I'm sorry. This has come as a surprise for you, but I have had top private investigators looking for Nimr for two years now and to suddenly have him so close—well, I wasn't sure what to do. I thought meeting you publicly through the hospital might be easier for you, but all I've done is barge into your life and upset you.'

She'd stepped away from his hand.

'I have to go,' she said, slipping behind him as he moved forward, escaping this time, though not for long.

He caught up with her by the time they'd reached the elevator.

'We need to talk!' he said, probably too loudly from the stares he got as they entered the already packed space.

She was pressed against him so he couldn't see her face, but the shake of her head, dark curls moving beneath his chin—brushing his skin—gave him his answer.

Soft dark curls from what he could see, giving off a hint of something he recognised but couldn't name.

Rosewater?

Back home, it was used in many local dishes—but in hair?

He breathed in the scent again as the elevator reached the ground floor—whatever it was that had stirred inside him earlier stirring again—and they led the exodus out into the corridor.

Expecting her to make a dash for some bolthole he'd never find in the big hospital, he caught her arm.

She spun towards him.

'I'll call Security,' she warned, but his mind was still on rosewater.

'Is it rosewater I can smell?'

The words were out before he considered how inappropriate they were.

'Rosewater?' she demanded, outrage warming her cheeks to a rosy pink. Grey eyes spitting fire, all fear gone. She probably had some kind of emergency call button somewhere on her person—

'I could smell rosewater,' he said, aware of how lame it sounded. 'The women use it in cooking at home.'

'The women, huh?' she said, but a lot of her tension was gone, and he kind of thought her soft pink lips might be trying hard not to smile.

Pleased they'd seemed to reach some kind of armistice, he raised both hands in surrender.

'I will *not* get into an argument with you about women's rights! I'm a believer in them myself. In fact, that's one of the reasons I'm so anxious to take Nimr home. My country needs to be dragged into the twenty-first century, and as his regent I could at least begin the task.'

She studied him for a moment, not bothering to hide the suspicion that had flared in her wide eyes.

'And you can't do that without him there—a boy of four? Surely, if you're related and next in line after him, you can get started without his presence.'

Malik sighed. He'd had a long journey, spent far too long convincing the finance man to arrange his meeting with this woman, thinking it was better to do it with an authority figure to introduce them—as it would have been at home. And now she was demanding answers to questions that could take hours to explain.

'I've got to get home,' she said, halting any further conversation. 'Joe goes to swimming training and I have to be there for Nim.'

'Nimr,' Malik corrected automatically, giving the 'r' on the end of his nephew's name the slight roll it required.

'Whatever!' his companion snapped. 'But we'll never

get through any conversation if you're going to correct his name every time I say it! And you know nothing about Australian kids if you imagine he could get through childhood with a rolled "r" on the end of his name without incessant teasing, so here he's Nim!'

And she stalked away, her anger back, and clearly seen in the straight shoulders and swift strides that somehow drew his attention to strong, shapely legs and a trim figure.

Kept his attention for an instant too long…

He sighed again.

He had more important matters at hand than a woman with grey eyes and a trim figure. Although Tariq had always been the practised negotiator—when he'd bothered—he, Malik, had stepped in often enough to be a competent one. But he'd blown it this time. He could understand her fighting him if she'd grown fond of the boy—that would be understandable—but part of her resistance had definitely been fear.

At least he knew where she lived.

In fear?

Rattled by the encounter, Lauren made her way out of the hospital by the nearest exit, finding herself in the wrong car park, so by the time she'd found her small vehicle she was shaking with the tension the stranger's appearance had generated.

Tension and fear—and something else, something she really didn't want to acknowledge.

She unlocked the door and slumped gratefully into the driving seat, opening windows and starting the air-conditioning as the vehicle, after standing in the summer sun all day, was like an inferno. Even the steering wheel was too hot to touch, so the idea of resting her forearms on it and having a wee cry had to be denied.

Not that she'd let that man make her cry! She'd shed

enough tears four years ago—enough to last a lifetime. Although admittedly there'd been more, when Nim had been a baby and, teething or not well, impossible to settle, she'd felt totally alone.

Then Aunt Jane had sold her parents' house for her, found the duplex for them on the other side of the country, set up the security, and made it safe enough for her to finally give Nim a home.

It was time to get home to her son. She couldn't let Joe down. Without Joe she'd be lost, she *and* Nim.

And no matter what that man said, Nim was hers and hers he was going to stay. He could grow up as an ordinary Australian boy and need never know much at all about that strange place thousands of miles away where his birth mother had lost her bearings.

Oh, *Lily*.

With a huff of impatience at the sudden sense of loss inside her, she drove out of the parking area and headed for home, her mind back on practical matters.

Did she have to stop at the shops for fruit for Nim's lunchbox tomorrow or had Joe called in on his way back from kindy?

He probably had and she couldn't think of anything else they needed.

Except perhaps a magic carpet to whisk Sheikh whoever he was back to where he'd come from. But magic carpets were fairly rare in Abbotsfield, for all it was a thriving regional city.

Regional city?

How *had* the man found her here, thousands of miles from where she'd grown up in Perth? All the police reports on the so-called accident had put the family's place of residence as Perth. And after that she'd disappeared. The family's assets had been frozen so she'd borrowed enough from Aunt Jane to buy the campervan, and she and tiny baby Nim had lived like gypsies, moving constantly, she doing anything to keep him safe.

Lauren's mind was lost in the past and, driving on auto-pilot, it was only as she was using the remote to open the outer gate that she saw the sleek black luxury vehicle parked outside.

The fear she'd felt earlier turned to terror and she dropped the remote as if it would burn her fingers. She parked behind the ominous car, only too aware of who would be inside it.

Or inside her house?

Dear heaven, surely not!

She shot from her car, and strode towards the limo, hauling open the driver's door so suddenly a slim man in a blue suit and matching cap almost fell out, his cap coming askew on his head.

'Who are you and what are you doing here?" she demanded, hoping Joe was inside with one finger poised above the alarm.

'He's my driver. He owns the hire car.'

Sheikh whatever was emerging from the back seat on the passenger side. 'I had no time to waste finding my way around your city, small though it might be.'

'Oh, and I suppose *your* city is ginormous!' Lauren shot at him, and immediately regretted it as this wasn't the argument she should be having.

Especially as the wretched man had the nerve to smile.

Well, she supposed it was a smile—he'd definitely moved his lips and revealed a dazzling array of perfectly aligned white teeth, but it was a crocodile that came to mind rather than rapprochement.

'Would you feel easier discussing the situation here?" he continued, as smooth as custard.

'There is no situation to discuss,' she said, hoping she sounded a lot more determined than she felt. Seeing the man who might just be a murderer standing outside her home had brought back all her fear, yet in some offbeat section of her brain she was simply seeing the man.

Bizarre, to say the least.

It wasn't as if she didn't see dozens of men every day, but this was definitely not that kind of seeing.

He'd taken off his suit jacket and rolled up his sleeves a little to reveal smooth olive skin that gleamed in the sunlight, while his shirt clung to a body she guessed had been shaped through exercise—not too much, just enough to give definition to hard pecs and wide shoulders beneath the snowy-white material.

She wouldn't look at his neck, rising from the now tieless shirt—well, only to see it as a strong column…

Ye gods! What was the matter with her? She was standing in the street mooning over a man who was undoubtedly her enemy?

'I don't want you in my house,' she finally said, meaning, I don't want you anywhere near me, not now, not ever, but especially not now when I'm so damned confused I can't think straight.

Fortunately, Joe appeared in the doorway at that moment, preceded by Ghost, Joe's pale German shepherd, and with Nim no doubt right behind, probably peering through Joe's legs, for all he was supposed to stay inside when people came.

'The gentleman's just leaving,' Lauren said, speaking to Joe but with her eyes on the Sheikh.

'We need to talk,' he said to her. 'It's imperative. I will not invade the sanctity of your home—' was there a 'not right now' hovering behind the words? '—but I shall call for you at seven.'

'Get into a car with a stranger? I think not! If we do need to talk, then we can talk at your hotel. Where are you staying?'

'The Regal.'

Lauren nodded.

'I'll meet you there at eight,' she said, hoping she'd spoken loftily enough for him to assume she dined at The Regal regularly, and at the same time wondering desperately what she might have in her wardrobe that she could wear to such a place. And whether Joe would be back from training, or, if not, there was always Aunt Jane who'd stand in…

The Sheikh nodded graciously, before pointing a finger at the gathering in the doorway.

'Security's a little lax. I could have shot the dog, then the nanny, and grabbed the boy.'

'You wouldn't!' Lauren whispered, then slid limply to the ground, a black cloud closing over her as the events of the afternoon finally caught up with her.

Joe darted forward but Malik was there first, lifting Lauren into his arms and marching towards the front door, telling the dog to sit in such a firm voice it dropped to his haunches.

'Get a cool, wet cloth,' he said to the so-called nanny. 'It's just a faint. I can feel her coming round already, so I'd better put her down because if she realises it's me holding her she's likely to hit me.'

'You can put her on the couch,' a small boy said, his eyes wide with unshed tears as he saw his mother in such a helpless state.

'She'll be better soon,' Malik assured the boy who was, without doubt, Nimr, for he was the dead spit of Tariq at that age.

Tariq, the brother Malik had worshipped all his young life and followed around like a puppy.

'Here!'

The nanny had returned, and the hoarseness in his voice made Malik turn to look at him—to see a face distorted by the scars of operations that had somehow put it back together.

'I am Malik,' he said, holding out his hand.

'That's Joe,' Nimr said, looking up from where he was wiping his mother's face with the damp hand towel. 'Joe looks after us.'

'I noticed that,' Malik told the boy, although his eyes were on the mother now—Lauren—dark lashes fluttering against her cheeks as she slowly became aware of her surroundings. Something that wasn't entirely guilt fluttered inside him, moved by her paleness—her vulnerability...

Her eyes opened, deep grey pools of fear and confusion—and *he* had caused the fear, first by arriving as he had and then with his foolish words about their protection.

Although that part was deadly serious. If there really was a threat against his nephew, he'd be better off back in Madan.

He should take the boy home, no matter what.

She sat up so suddenly he was knocked from where he crouched by the couch, landing awkwardly on his butt.

At least it gave Nimr a laugh.

'You're in my house!'

Outrage vied with disbelief as Lauren took in this man's presence. He was so close she could hardly not notice that his eyes were not the black she'd thought them but a surprising warm toffee colour, and right now were looking intently at her.

'You have to go,' she said, unable to tell if her hyperawareness of him—the unsettled feeling in her chest—was to do with the shock she'd had or the man himself.

Whatever it was, she wanted it gone too.

He hesitated, aware of the nanny standing behind him, ready to break him in two if he so much as touched the recovering woman.

He moved back a little, and said gently, 'I'm sorry, but we do have to talk, and I think the sooner the better.'

Lauren forced her fuzzy brain to sort out the words, and one thing became perfectly clear. This man was not leaving until he'd said what he'd come to say.

And considering that, wouldn't it be better to listen to him here and now—well, not right now as she had to get Nim's dinner, her own dinner, too, given that lunch had been a snatched apple and cup of coffee and her stomach was making her aware that she was famished.

She heaved herself upright on the sofa, Nim slipping up to sit beside her and take her hand.

'I'm all right,' she assured him. 'I just forgot to have my lunch and that's what made me faint like that.'

Lying to her son? She knew full well it was the man's suggestion that it would have been easy to abduct Nim that had made her mind shut down.

Which left her with the man—the Madani man!

He was standing back—against a window once again—and, much as she hated having him in her house, she knew she wouldn't be rid of him until she'd listened to what he'd come to say.

'I have to give Nim his dinner and I usually eat with him so you might as well stay and eat with us. That way we can talk when Nim's gone to bed. I'll just have a quick wash—Nim, you need to wash your hands for dinner so you come with me.'

'You get off to training,' she added to Joe, who was standing, watching them all. 'I'm fine now and I'll have an early night.'

She was leaving the room when she remembered the big black car parked outside her yard, and added to Malik, 'You'd better get your driver and bring him in for dinner too.'

'The driver?'

He sounded so incredulous, Lauren almost laughed.

'Drivers do eat, you know,' she said. 'And there's plenty so it's hardly fair to leave him sitting out there.'

Well, she hoped there was plenty…

'Please go out and invite him in.'

Wondering if this was a quirk of democracy in this country or because the woman didn't want to be alone with him, Malik went, returning with the driver, who'd protested he was quite okay and happy to wait without food.

But already aware that he was dealing with a stubborn woman, Malik had insisted.

He found the woman in question bent double over a large chest freezer, pulling out various plastic-wrapped containers and muttering to herself.

'We're having shepherd's pie,' Nimr announced. 'It's my turn to choose and it's my favourite.'

Malik looked at the boy he knew yet didn't know and felt pain stab into his heart.

'Oh, yes?' he said. 'Do you make it out of shepherds?'

The boy laughed.

'No, silly! Mum makes it with meat, and puts potato on the top, and it's yummy and you don't have to cut it up so it's easy to eat.'

Malik smiled at the boy, feeling a weird kind of pleasure that the child had offered him this small confidence.

'Ha, knew I had one!'

The triumphant cry from the freezer had them moving into the kitchen where their pink-cheeked hostess, apparently fully recovered from her faint, had emerged from the freezer in triumph.

Seeing the two men, the driver trying to hide behind the door, her cheeks went a deeper pink.

'Sorry,' she said. 'I tend to cook a lot on my days off,

and I always make different sizes of each dish for when Joe's here—'

'And when Joe and Aunt Jane both come,' Nim finished for her, turning to the visitors to hold up four fingers. 'That's four, you see, and tonight it's four too.'

Perhaps embarrassed by her son's delight in the visitors, his mother had stripped layers of plastic from the frozen dish and set it going in the microwave. And with her back resolutely turned to the two men, she was peeling carrots and cutting chunks of broccoli off a large green head.

Wishing it was my head, no doubt, Malik thought, as she slashed the knife down.

Her shoulders rose as he watched and he knew she was taking a deep breath.

After which, she turned towards her visitors and said quietly, 'It will be half an hour. Would you like to wait in the living room? Perhaps you'd like a glass of cold water?'

'Thank you,' Malik said, then aware of the driver lurking behind him, remembered his manners.

'This is my driver, Peter—'

'Cross,' their hostess finished for him, stepping forward and, to Malik's surprise, giving the man a hug.

'Oh, sorry, Peter, I hadn't realised it was you I made fall out of the car. How's Susie?'

The man held up crossed fingers.

'So far, so good, Lauren. You know how it goes.'

'I do indeed,' Lauren told him. 'Now, a glass of water, each of you?'

'That'd be lovely,' Peter said, and well aware that he'd lost what little conversational control he might have had, Malik agreed, following the other man back into the living room.

It was Nimr who brought the water, two tall glasses balanced on a round tray.

Malik took his, thanked the boy, and wondered what on earth one said to start a conversation with a four-year-old.

Not that he needed to worry, for the boy sat down on the sofa next to the driver and, easily adopting the role of host, turned to Malik to explain.

'Susie's my best friend at kindy. She's been sick. She wears cute hats because she's got no hair. No one minds she's got no hair anyway, and when she first had no hair we all shaved our heads, even the girls, to show it was okay, but she wears the hats because she likes them.'

Malik turned to Peter, who was smiling at the boy.

'Leukaemia?' he asked quietly.

A nod in reply, and, although knowing many of the childhood variants of leukaemia had a high rate of recovery, Malik didn't want to probe too deeply.

Particularly as the earlier conversation and the man's crossed fingers now made sense. Susie must be in remission at the moment, and Malik knew only too well the tightrope parents walked at such times.

'And we have rabbits at kindy too,' Nimr announced. 'Sometimes in the holidays some of the kids get to take them home but Mum says we can't because she has to work and Joe can't be expected to look after a rabbit *and* me.'

Malik hid a smile. The boy was obviously repeating his mother's words, but his aggrieved tone left his listeners in no doubt about his opinion of this edict.

'Do you have rabbits?' he asked.

Malik shook his head.

'No rabbits, but we do have many interesting animals where I live, and many dogs that are tall and run very fast and are called saluki hounds.'

Nimr seemed to ponder this information for a moment, then said knowledgably, 'Hound is another name for a dog. I like dogs, but—'

Malik was pretty sure he was about to hear Mum's opinion of keeping a dog when they were called into the kitchen for dinner. Considering it was little over an hour since she'd fainted in the gateway, Sister Lauren Macpherson had done a sterling job.

The small wooden table had a blue bowl of flowers in the middle of it and four places neatly set, with water glasses in front of each place.

Nimr had gone in front of them and lifted a tall, plastic jug of water from the refrigerator.

'See how strong I am,' he said, holding it a little higher.

'But not quite strong enough to pour,' his mother said, as she saved the tilting jug and filled the water glasses.

'Maybe when I'm five,' Nimr said, climbing onto what must be his accustomed chair.

He was a confident young man, Malik realised, and polite as well. His work as a paediatrician had brought him into contact with countless children, and he'd learned to appreciate the ones with good manners and the quiet confidence he sensed in the boy.

And something very likeable.

He tried to think back to when he and Tariq had been children, but suspected that Tariq had probably not been likeable even then.

Lovable, yes!

He, Malik, had adored him, as had their mother, but he'd been a tease, daring his brother to do things that they'd known were wrong, laughing when Malik had refused.

Was it that challenge to try everything—good or bad—that had led him to drugs, or simply the jet-setting lifestyle he'd led from his late teens, money giving him the freedom their restricted upbringing had denied them?

CHAPTER TWO

THE MEAL WAS simple but delicious, and, perhaps sensing an atmosphere he didn't understand, it was his driver who kept the conversation going, with considerable help from the boy, who was happy to join in on any subject.

Although, Malik realised rather sadly, the man was steering the conversation so the boy could join in, no doubt because he had a child of the same age.

He was wondering how he'd react to children of his own—certainly he'd never experienced a meal like this as a child of Nimr's age. He'd still have been eating with the women and listening to their high-pitched chatter and gossip—

'Now, I think Sheikh Madani wishes to talk with your mother, young Nim, and Joe's still at training, so how about I do your bath and bedtime story?'

Peter Cross's words had broken into Malik's memories, and Nimr was already excusing himself from the table, only too willing to have someone different supervising his bedtime routine.

'Thanks, Peter,' his hostess said, confirming Malik's suspicions that the man was a close family friend.

Through their children or through the hospital?

He didn't ask as Lauren was speaking again.

'I'll just rinse off these dishes and stack the dishwasher and be with you shortly.'

'I can rinse dishes,' Malik said, stacking dirty plates together, before standing up and carrying them to the sink.

He read the surprise on her face, and couldn't help adding, 'Don't judge me by my brother,' before setting to work on his task, rinsing the plates and passing them to Lauren—he had to get used to calling her that in his mind—to stack into place.

She was silent as she worked, but as she shut the door of the machine and set it to wash, she said quietly, 'I didn't know him well—your brother, I mean. He'd barely arrived in Australia when the—the accident happened.'

Which made him wonder if he'd spoken too harshly.

He sought to make amends.

'I've often wondered if I knew him at all,' he told her, 'although as children we were inseparable.'

'It's because Nim doesn't have a brother—or even a sister—that I like him to go to kindy where he can play with other children, and he's so looking forward to going to school next year.'

'Aren't we all,' a deep, slightly fractured voice said, and Malik turned to see Joe in the doorway, back from wherever he had been.

'Peter tells me you're wanted in the bedroom for a goodnight kiss,' he said to Lauren, who, to Malik's considerable surprise, said quietly, 'Perhaps you'd like to say goodnight, too.'

'Joe and I have things to discuss about the new boys' club we want to set up in the community centre, so we'll talk in the kitchen,' Peter said as they met in the short passage. 'Would you like us to bring coffee in to you and the Sheikh?'

* * *

Lauren shook her head.

This was all getting far too matey, in her opinion, but she was thankful the two men would be there.

'Do they worry about you, that they are staying close?' her guest asked, as they walked towards the boy's bedroom.

'I doubt that, but they know it would be wrong of them to leave me here with a stranger.'

'You have loyal friends,' he said with a smile, and that was a mistake. Not the smile, which was warm and slightly teasing, but the way it made her feel.

Tingles from a smile?

For pity's sake, this was the man who had quite possibly killed her entire family—except for Nim.

Yet she'd been conscious of that inner—what, tension?— from the moment she'd first seen him and wondered if that's how Tariq had made Lily feel...

Stupid! That's what it was.

Especially as the man wanted to take her child...

She opened the door into the bedroom, but the excitement of the visitors had meant she'd left it too late to get her goodnight kiss.

But she could leave one, and she leant over the child she loved with all her heart and kissed him gently on his cheek.

She turned to the man who stood watching in the doorway.

'He'll be sorry to have missed you,' she said quietly, but knew he hadn't heard her. He was watching the sleeping boy and the sadness she read in his eyes was almost more than she could stand.

She slipped past him, heading for the living room, aware he was following her, horribly aware of *him*.

She took the armchair and waved the man towards the not-very-comfortable sofa, which had been cheap and had very quickly taken to the shape of her and Nim's posteriors so no one else's quite seemed to fit it.

And she wouldn't think about his posterior either...

'So talk!' she said, determined to find out exactly what he wanted. Why he'd come. She knew he'd come for Nim, but she wanted to know why.

'Do you know much about Madan?'

The question, when it finally came, surprised her, as he'd seemed more like a man who'd cut to the chase and she knew the chase, in this case, was Nim.

'I know the usual stuff from the internet. It's a small country, with enough oil beneath its sands to make it wealthy. Incredibly wealthy, if the way Tariq threw money around was any indication. I know my sister hated it, preferring to spend her time jet-setting around the world to glitzy hotels and ultra-trendy resorts—to wherever there was a party going on. Although, to be fair, that all stopped once she became pregnant.'

She watched the man as she spoke, and saw his face darken, but when he spoke she could hear regret, and also love, in his voice.

'My brother was not a wise man.'

Lauren waited. He was here for a reason, so it was his story to tell.

He began slowly. 'My father, in his declining years, was also not wise. His mind weakened and he began to listen to those around him—to listen to advice that would benefit the speaker but not the country. He had governed well but strictly, refusing to allow the new-found wealth of the country to change it.'

A pause, before he added rather bitterly, 'In any way!'

'And his advisors?' Lauren asked when the man had sat in brooding silence for a few moments.

'Advised stupidity. Advised progress, but far too quickly for the land or the people to handle. We are the keepers of our land, our settlement built around a large oasis so for many, many centuries we have been an important place on the trading routes that cross from Asia to Europe.'

'Like the Silk Road—I've read so much about that, it's such an ancient highway.'

Malik nodded.

'Traders followed the routes, but they required new supplies of food, and sometimes shelter, always new animals—camels and sheep—to replace those they lost along the way. So really our people are farmers and shopkeepers—that has been their role for generation after generation.'

'And it's changed how?'

He didn't need to look at the woman to see her interest. It charged her voice, and something deep inside him whispered a small hope.

Maybe this sister would be different…

'In the beginning, the oil men who held the leases built a hotel for their senior staff and guests, and an air terminal and runways for their planes. Then my father and his friends took this as progress—as the way to go. They built a bigger hotel and an airline company. And more hotels and shopping malls, all the things they thought a desert city might need to attract the tourist dollars, but—'

'You feel money would be better spent on other things? On things that benefit your own people, not the tourists.'

He nodded.

'Hospitals and schools, a university and training colleges. With health and education our people can go anywhere, do anything. They can become the doctors and the architects and engineers of the new Madan. They can build a city for them and their families, a city *they* would want to live in.'

'And a shopping mall doesn't cut it?' she said with a smile. But she'd heard the real passion in his voice, and understood his desire to give his people the skills to live in this new world—*their* new world.

Would Tariq have felt the same?

But something told her that this man had a deep integrity his brother had lacked, and admiration for him joined the whatever else it was that had been going on inside her…

'So, where does Nim come into this?'

He didn't answer immediately—this man whose name meant Protector of the King.

Did he see it as his duty to protect Nim or did he want him for reasons of his own?

'The country will, one day, be under Nimr's rule, so he needs to grow up there, to learn the history and know the people. But until he comes of age, which is twenty-two in Madan, the head of state will be his regent.'

'Which is you?'

He shook his head.

'Not necessarily. As the closest relative, yes, it should be my position, but you must understand that until my father died less than a year ago, I had assumed Nimr had been killed in the accident.'

'But surely someone—your father—would have received a report? The investigation from the police, the coroner's office, along with the inquest results, all took for ever, I know, but he'd have seen the final reports, surely?'

He nodded.

'There were many reports,' he said, 'but none that I had seen until after my father's death and I was going through his papers. It was then I realised the child had survived, and began my search for him.'

'And *found* us!'

'Just so!' Malik said, then those observant eyes studied her for a few moments, before he added, 'I would never harm either you or Nimr, you must believe that. I did not kill my brother and your family, but I have sworn to find out who did, and I shall.'

He paused, but she'd heard both the commitment and determination in his voice.

'But that is for the future,' he continued, while she wondered why she believed him—she who had trusted so few people in the last four years.

Think about it later, she told herself, turning her attention back to his words—his explanations.

'I cannot afford the time to make it a priority. Right now, my country needs strong rule—a plan for the future and immediate direction. As Nimr's regent—if the child is *seen* to be in my care—I can appoint people who will provide that. I'll have to do a certain level of official business, but I am a doctor, not a politician, and once I have the right people in place, I can return to my job at the hospital, such as it is.'

'So you want to take my son?' Lauren said, her voice shaking with the tension she was feeling. The man had made a valid argument, and he was as closely related to Nim as she was. Except—

'Except you can't!' she said. 'I've adopted him and he's legally mine. I'm quite sure there must be someone—yourself, no doubt—who's the next in line after him. Take the reins yourself or use someone you trust. Let Nim grow up an ordinary Aussie boy.'

'Surrounded by security and with you living in fear of what might happen to him?' Malik snapped. 'Do you not understand I would protect him with my life? Do you not believe that? But I cannot do it while he is here.'

She *did* understand him—the passion in his voice as he'd spoken of his country had been very real, but...

'You're just being stubborn,' she told him. 'Can't you see that if someone else becomes ruler, Nim will no longer matter? He will no longer need protection of any kind because your successors or those of whoever you get to rule the land will follow on. People will forget he ever existed.'

'Nimr, the son of Tariq, will never be forgotten, not in my heart, and not in the hearts of my people.'

'But your people don't know of his existence!' Lauren argued. 'He was born here—he was only two weeks old when his parents were killed. Even before that, Lily had determined to divorce Tariq, to settle down here in Australia.'

'And you could see that happening?' the aggravating man demanded. 'The beautiful butterfly settling anywhere?'

There was no way that Lauren was going to admit she shared his doubts about her sister—or *her* doubts about Lily leaving Tariq?

'That's beside the point,' she said. 'I cannot believe that there is no way you can help your country without dragging a four-year-old boy along behind you.'

'He would *not* be *behind* me, he would be King. I would be nothing more than his regent—a caretaker for the country until he comes of age.'

It was all far too complicated, but the idea of Nim being some kind of figurehead to be paraded at will was just too much for her to take in.

'Well, I'm sorry. I understand you mean well, and that you want what is best for your country, but I have to think about my son, and his welfare, and his future.'

'And you think that's here? Surrounded by security all his life, and not very effective security at that?'

Her earlier moment of absolute terror flashed before her eyes and she had to hold back a gasp. But she couldn't show more weakness, not to this man...

'Joe opened that door for *me*, and it would have been obvious to him that I knew you—or at least knew who you were. If you'd approached on your own it would have been a different story.'

It sounded weak even to her own ears.

'And he'll be there with Nimr when he plays in the park with his friends from school? How long will a boy put up with that kind of shadow? How long before he gets embarrassed about it, and finds ways of avoiding Joe's protection?'

He was giving voice to the thoughts that kept Lauren awake most nights and she hid the dread they brought.

'I'm not stupid!' she snapped. 'Lily's stories about people conspiring to get rid of her and Tariq, which I'd thought gross exaggerations, were proven to be true. And I've always known I could only go so far to protect Nim. But after four years I'd begun to hope that anyone who actually knew of his existence would have forgotten about him.'

Those conversations—well, them and the accident and abduction—were the reasons Lauren had fled. With help from the police liaison officer, she'd officially changed her name and disappeared, moving constantly for the first two years—in touch with the police in different places who had twice alerted her that someone from Madan was looking for them—never entirely sure they were safe.

And now Lily's words were coming true. Now this man was here, wanting to take her child—*Lily's* child.

'I'm sorry,' she said. 'I'm sure you mean well, but I have to think of Nim, so no more talk. He's not going—*we're* not going—anywhere.'

Except to move as soon as possible to another town, maybe a city... Would a city be easier to lose themselves in? Even with half the money from the sale of her parents' mansion put away for Nim, she still had more than enough to take them anywhere in the world.

But the thought of moving again made her feel ill. Aunt Jane and Joe were settled in the other half of the duplex,

They'd done more than enough for her and Nim already, and weren't even true family, for all Aunt Jane had been her mother's best friend, and Joe had worshipped Lily since they were children—

'*What* did you say?'

She shook her head to clear it, realising it was tiredness that had led her mind to stray away from this man—from danger.

He was watching her, his face devoid of expression, but his eyes were focussed.

Seeking her reaction?

'I said I would prefer not to go through official channels, but by the law of *my* country Nimr became *my* child on the death of his father. I have every right in law to claim him.'

Lauren ran her tongue over suddenly dry lips, tried to think, but shock and anger, and possibly exhaustion, had closed her brain.

Malik saw what little colour she'd had in her cheeks fade, and the tip of her tongue slide across her pale lips.

And found himself wanting nothing more than to take care of her—this small, fiercely protective woman. Not only to keep her safe but to lift the burden of fear from her slim shoulders.

To hold her, tell her it would all work out.

To hold her?

Get your mind back on the job.

But guilt at how he'd hurt her with his words made him reach out and touch one small, cold hand, where it lay in her lap.

'I'm sorry, I shouldn't have threatened you like that— you look exhausted, and all this has been a shock to you. No one should make decisions when they're tired, but there's a way out of this for all of us. Don't answer now, we will talk again in the morning. I shall phone your Mr Marshall and explain you won't be in to work.'

But she'd obviously stopped listening earlier in his conversation.

'A way out for all of us?' she asked, looking at him with a thousand questions in her lovely eyes.

'Of course,' he told her, and felt a small spurt of unexpected excitement even thinking about his solution.

'We shall get married,' he announced. 'That way Nim is both of ours and will be doubly protected.'

Her eyes had widened and although he hadn't thought she could get any paler, she was now sheet-white.

But she stood up, and for a moment he thought she might physically attack him, but in the end she glared at him and said, 'You must be mad!' before turning towards the kitchen.

'Peter, your customer is ready to leave,' she called, before disappearing down the passage, presumably into her bedroom.

As his driver appeared, with Joe looming behind him, Malik realised there was no point in arguing, but the idea, which had come to him out of nowhere, was brilliant.

All he had to do was convince Lauren.

Her name rolled a little on his tongue and, inside his head, he tried it out a few times.

He said goodnight to Joe, and followed Peter out to the car, but his mind, for once, was not on Nimr, but on the woman he'd decided to marry…

CHAPTER THREE

SHEER EXHAUSTION BLOCKED Lauren's mind so no matter how hard she tried to think about Malik's ridiculous proposal, her brain refused to work.

She went into Nim's room and sat on the edge of his bed, a place where peace and contentment usually washed over her. But not tonight. Tonight all she saw was a little boy she'd sworn to protect, a little boy she loved with all her heart.

Brushing his cheek with one last goodnight kiss, she took herself to bed. Bed was a good place to think!

It was no good. The man's arrival, her fainting when she never fainted, the fact that he knew where they lived—the jumble of thoughts was too much to untangle, and that was without the marriage bit.

Contrary to all her expectations, her mind shut down on it all and she slept, well and deeply, until Nim bounced into her bed at seven the next morning.

He was full of the joys another day might bring; so happy and loving as he snuggled down with her, she thought her heart might stop.

She put her arms around him and drew him closer, breathing in the little-boy smell of him, remembering the man—Malik—talking about rosewater, the scent of her shampoo…

'What's with you two this morning?'

Joe's call from the front of the house reminded her it was a workday, and already she was well behind schedule. Nim was gone, off to greet Joe, but Lauren made it out of bed, then stood uncertainly beside it.

Was Malik going ahead and arranging time off for her this morning?

No, she was sure she hadn't agreed to that! But what had she agreed to?

Definitely not to his ridiculous idea that they marry.

Go to work, that's what she'd do, and once there she'd have no time to think of anything but her patients…

She had a quick shower to freshen up, put on a clean uniform, and by the time she could smell bacon sizzling in the pan, she was ready for the day ahead.

A *normal* day ahead!

Until Joe looked her up and down, glanced towards the calendar on the fridge and said, 'I thought you were working the late shift today.'

Of course she was! Two to ten, and Joe would know because he missed his training on late-shift evenings.

'Forgot,' she mumbled as she sat down to her bacon and eggs, a treat Joe cooked for them about once a week.

'Can we have this every day, Mum?' Nim asked, and she shook her head.

'You know it's a Joe special,' she reminded Nim, 'and anyway, cereal will make you strong.'

But Nim had already forgotten the argument. He was peering out the kitchen door, and through the living room where a window revealed a long black limousine pulling up outside.

'It looks like Susie's dad's car,' he said. 'Do you think he might drive me to school in it?'

Rendered speechless by the thought of who might be in

the hire car, Lauren was saved answering by a long peal of the doorbell.

'I'll go,' Joe said, and the words brought Lauren back to panic mode.

'Check who's out there before you open the door,' she reminded him, totally unnecessarily, but at least she'd managed to speak.

'And, Nim, run along to your bedroom and get dressed or you'll be late for kindy.'

Once she had Joe and Nim out of the house, perhaps she'd be able to think clearly.

She smiled to herself.

She was ready for work—a ready-made excuse not to talk to the man. *Hello and goodbye, sorry I can't stop...*

She guessed it was only putting off the inevitable, but it would give her time to think.

Then he was there, taller than she remembered, and so darned good-looking in a casual polo shirt and pale chinos that she hoped she wasn't gaping at him.

'I was told you are not on duty until later,' he said by way of greeting. 'I contacted Mr Marshall to explain we had more business to discuss, and ask if it was possible for you to have some time off, and he explained.'

Lauren closed her eyes and swore to herself. Mr Marshall was no doubt toadying up to someone he thought might have money to give away. He'd found where she was working the previous day so had probably had no trouble checking her roster.

But a uniform was a bit like armour. It made you a stronger person. Or so she told herself when she realised he'd foiled her planned escape and she'd *have* to talk to him.

Joe was ushering the visitor into the living room, offering coffee, although he and Nim should be leaving for kindy.

Lauren followed, trying to convince herself the uniform

as armour idea hadn't worked the previous evening because it had been rumpled and grubby…

She sat down and wondered what to do next. If Joe hadn't offered coffee, she could have done that and escaped into the kitchen, but apparently her visitor refused coffee for Joe was in Nim's bedroom, putting on his shoes, from the sound of things, urging him to hurry or they'd be late.

'Would you want to bring Joe?'

The question was so bamboozling, it forced Lauren into speech.

'Would I want to bring Joe where?' she asked.

'To Madan, of course.'

He didn't actually add 'you idiot', but Lauren heard it hovering at the end of the words.

'You're not making sense,' she said.

And he smiled.

Uniforms weren't good armour against smiles. For some unfathomable reason, that smile had melted something inside her—something hard and unrelenting that had taken her four years to build.

'When we marry,' he was saying now, as if everything had been settled in some glitch in time, and they were moving on to the next stage of their lives.

'When we *marry*?' she echoed, but heard a traitorous tremor in her voice and sat up straighter, shoring up the defences that smile had fractured. 'I haven't agreed to marry you!'

That was better—her voice was stronger.

Another smile, but this one she was ready for, steeled herself against it…

'Oh, but you will, when you've had time to take it in, and realise it's the best solution for all of us.'

He paused, and she felt his scrutiny.

'You're still tired, and you do need time, but I have to leave and want to make all the arrangements before I go.

You will need passports, of course, for you and Nimr. But back to where we started, do you want to bring Joe with you?'

Lauren shook her head.

It was useless arguing with the man, he simply did not listen, and to keep repeating that she hadn't agreed to marry him was pointless.

'Go away,' she said. 'You're right, I'm not on duty until late. I could meet you for an early lunch at twelve. We could talk then.'

Somewhere neutral, not here in her home—the home that had once been a safe haven for her and Nim but now felt more like a battleground.

He was talking again, suggesting The Regal once more, telling her he'd send Peter to collect her.

'And drive me home from work late in the evening?' she snapped. 'I will make my own arrangements, thank you. I will see you at twelve.'

And she stood up so he would know his visit was over.

Except that Nim came bounding out to greet the visitor, who touched the boy's head so gently Lauren felt her defences begin to crumble again.

She kissed her little boy goodbye, and wondered if she'd been fooling herself in thinking she could keep him safe. Then they were all gone, Nim having won a lift in the limo. Lauren slumped down on the sofa, stretched out on her back, and looked up at the ceiling, which was as blank as her mind…

Malik felt strangely satisfied as they drove away from the small duplex, the man called Joe silent beside him, Nim in the front seat, chattering away to Peter about cars he'd ridden in.

He'd learned more of Joe from Peter on his way back to the hotel. A decorated soldier, badly wounded, a left-leg amputee, although Malik hadn't picked up on that just from seeing the man move.

A family friend more than a relation, Peter had thought, Joe lived in the flat next door with his mother, training for some games for wounded service people, Peter had heard.

So Lauren had chosen her 'nanny' well, although he, Malik, sensed from her reaction to his appearance at the hospital that she had been starting to believe they were safe.

And that in itself was enough to strengthen his determination to take Nimr home to Madan. Whoever had killed his brother had waited until he was out of the country, where such an assassination would barely raise a ripple in Madan itself.

The knowledge that Tariq had died had saddened his people, but most were unaware of the violence of his death, and certainly not aware of the Australian police's suspicions that it had been murder.

But the fact remained that *someone* had killed Tariq, and that person could still go after Nimr, especially as now, a year after his father's death—the end of the mourning period—that the succession had to be formalised.

They'd pulled up outside the school, and the small boy, so like his father, reached over the seat to shake his hand and say goodbye. Joe nodded a farewell, and they were gone, Joe accompanying the boy right inside the building.

But Malik barely saw them go, his mind caught up in where his thoughts had led. What if whoever had killed Tariq was inside the palace itself?

Wasn't that the most likely answer?

And in that case, taking the boy there could be playing into that person or persons' hands. The palace with its labyrinthine corridors and upward of a hundred staff, who would know which person might wish, or be paid, to harm the boy?

'Back to their home,' he said to Peter, knowing that he

needed to get things settled right away. He had his mother's legacy, the huge house she'd built when his father had married his second wife. They'd go there. He'd staff it with people loyal only to him. Loyalty was part of his culture—his people had only survived because they trusted one another and would fight to the death against anyone who threatened one of their own.

He probably wouldn't tell Lauren that part in the argument he intended to put to her.

Back at her residence, he considered asking Peter to accompany him inside so Lauren wouldn't feel threatened, but the place was small, and even from the kitchen he was fairly certain his words would be overheard.

He could do this—*would* do this, *had* to do this!

He knew she was checking him through the spyhole before opening the door, knew she hadn't expected him to return, for she'd changed into white shorts and a red tank top. With her slim, tanned legs and small bare feet, she looked little more than a child herself, and for a moment he hesitated.

Should he rethink his plan?

Then he remembered the small boy, offering his hand to be shaken, saying goodbye, and knew his way was best.

She led him wordlessly back into the living room and subsided into a chair.

He followed her, took the damnably uncomfortable sofa, and drew a deep breath.

'I know you would like more time to think through my offer, but I realised, as we drove Nimr to his kindergarten, that I may have put you both in more danger just by being here.'

He paused, aware of the tension he'd caused with his words but needing to get them said.

'If I could find you, so could others, and while they may

have taken longer, I may also have unwittingly led them to you. You will need a passport, of course—'

'I have a passport—and Nim is on it. At one time I thought we might go to New Zealand, but I hardly see—'

'New Zealand would never have been far enough away from someone who wished harm to Nimr. In Madan I can keep you both safe.'

Even as he said the words, he knew it was somehow important to him that this woman stay as safe as the child...

Lauren stared at him—the bit about New Zealand not being far enough kept echoing in her head. It had always been in her mind as a last resort.

New Zealand had always *seemed* safe...

And if it wasn't?

'But why the marriage?' she asked. 'Could we not just go with you and live there? I could get work and Nim could go to school, like normal people.'

He shook his head.

'You would be living in my home—not the palace—and that would be unseemly for an unmarried woman. It need be marriage in name only, but only if we are married, and Nimr my son, can I keep you both safe.'

She ignored the shiver the word 'married' had given her, told herself she should feel relieved about the 'in name only' part of the conversation, but once again her brain was flooded with too much information and too many questions for her to think straight.

She must have been looking as lost as she felt because he said gently, 'I am sorry. This has been too great a shock for you to take in all at once. I have lived in torment that I could not save my beloved brother.'

He sighed before continuing, 'We, well, I, had thought he and Lily had split up, she returning to her family in Australia. Tariq had settled down, his wild lifestyle seemingly over. He was taking an interest in affairs of state and readying himself to take over from our father.'

Another pause, and Lauren could almost feel the anguish in Malik's soul.

'Then one day he was gone—out of the country, flying first to the United Kingdom, then the US. I was angry that he hadn't spoken to me or told me what he was doing. But for six months he'd been the perfect heir, the model Madani, and I had no suspicion he would end up in Australia. And no idea he was heading this way for the birth of his son.'

'You hadn't known Lily was pregnant?'

'No one did, not at home, I'm sure of that. And I suppose that hurts more than anything—that my brother, whom I loved for all we were so different, hadn't felt able to confide in me. Hadn't told me such joyous news…'

The pain in his voice pierced deep into Lauren's heart because she knew he'd carried it with him every day for four long years.

She wanted to say something—but what?

I'm sorry?

Too late—he was speaking again.

'Since he was killed, I've realised Tariq must have known he had an enemy and had sent Lily away for safety. When Nimr was born, he contacted our father to tell him the wonderful news, and two weeks later he was dead.'

'They were all dead—except for Nim,' Lauren reminded him, and he nodded, looking directly at her, his eyes burning with a fierce intensity.

'I have vowed to avenge them, Lauren, all of them. I will not kill their murderers, but I will find and punish them, I promise you.'

Lauren closed her eyes and tried to still her heart rate, to control whatever it was that fizzed along her nerves, for Malik hadn't finished his dramatic tale.

'My father was an old man even then, but he would not

have betrayed Tariq's trust. He would, though, not have been able to hide his delight and someone close to him guessed…'

'But why?'

It was the question she'd asked herself a thousand times four years ago, and, so far, had no answer.

'To be the leader of Madan is a powerful position in our land and neighbouring states. There is wealth, but many people have wealth now. It is the power of the position that some men crave.'

'The men who are building hotels instead of schools and hospitals?' Lauren asked, remembering their earlier conversation.

'Those, and others like them,' Malik told her. 'I know I am asking something almost impossible of you, but believe me when I say I would give my life for Nimr, and I ask that you trust me to take care of both of you.'

He paused, then added, 'I know I cannot prove my words and that I am asking you to put your faith in a stranger, but I swear, on my brother's name, that I will prove myself worthy of it.'

Lauren closed her eyes.

'I need to think,' she said, trying to put the pieces of the puzzle together. 'To start with, you said we won't be living in the palace, and I assume that means you think someone in the palace, close to your father, is the—enemy?'

It was totally ridiculous. Like a spy story, but even that didn't make sense. Not that anything much had made sense these last four years.

'But surely the people in the palace aren't prisoners? They can come and go? I'm sure no high-up person came to Australia to kill your brother—they would have sent someone. Can they not send someone to your home?'

She saw broad shoulders lift with a sigh, and looking at his face, saw the shadows beneath his eyes.

Perhaps he'd had less sleep than she had.

Perhaps he was genuinely very worried about all this…

'My home is staffed by my people who, as I have told you, would give their lives for me, or mine. Tariq was foolish to think distance would protect his family. It was far easier for whoever wanted him dead to have him killed in a foreign country. To kill him at home, there would have been a furore—accusations flying, suspicion everywhere, our police battling against age-old traditions of secrecy and conspiracy.'

'Which is why you feel it is safer for us to be there rather than here?'

Lauren hoped the shiver that ran down her spine wasn't echoed in her words.

'I believe it with all my heart,' he said, and although there were probably a hundred reasons why she *not* believe this man, she could sense the depth of passion in his words, and understood he'd loved his playboy brother as deeply as she'd loved her wayward sister…

And she'd heard the pain in his voice when he'd spoken of the wrongs being done in his country, and to its people, by those who put tourism and the money it might bring in above improving the health and education of the population. His commitment to a better future had shone through his words—he was doing this for Madan.

The words were powerful, but an even more powerful thought occurred to her. She got up and walked to the window, her mind tracking back through the conversation—his father dead, a year of mourning, now a succession to be settled…

There it was!

She'd had warnings the last two times someone had come from Madan, but not this time.

There had been no warning of this man's presence in the country, which could only mean the police no longer believed Nim was in danger. Yet with the succession in doubt, surely this was when he'd be in the most danger?

She clutched her stomach where fear ran rampant, and breathed deeply.

She had to think.

She returned to her chair, hoping her inner turmoil wasn't showing on her face.

'We'll go with you,' she said, and where she'd expected to feel dread she was surprised to find the words, once out, made her feel lighter, as if the burden she'd carried for four years had suddenly been lifted from her shoulders.

All the running, the phone calls to and from police, the checks in places as far apart as Coolgardie and Coober Pedy. And behind it all the sense of guilt that she'd never, for a minute, taken Lily's words of plots and murder seriously—never believed her own sister that such things could happen.

All of it over…

Don't be stupid, she warned herself. *You will still have to be wary and suspicious, careful whom you trust…*

But Malik had moved to stand in front of her. He bent and took her hand.

'I swear by all that is holy you will not regret that decision.'

His hand was warm, the palm firm, and he drew her to her feet so that she stood before him, close enough to smell his maleness, to feel the warmth of his body.

Then, to her astonishment, he kissed her lightly on the forehead, squeezed her fingers, and said, 'How long will it take you to pack?'

CHAPTER FOUR

DARNED MAN!

He'd walked out of her life again—well, out of her home—before she'd had time to register what he was saying, let alone throw up objections like having to give notice at work.

On the other hand, his being gone meant she could sit quietly and try to get her head around all that had happened in the last twenty-four hours. Except her mind refused to cooperate. It kept telling her it didn't know where to start thinking about it.

For a while, she just sat in her corner of the sofa and tried to relax. Only now her brain had found something it *could* think about—practicalities.

She'd have to get rid of the furniture before she could rent the flat—or should she rent it furnished?

No, there were things from her parents' home she didn't want to part with. Should she store them? Or leave the flat empty? She needed to talk to Aunt Jane—maybe Joe would like to live in the flat. *Aunt Jane*?

What on earth was she going to tell her?

And if she was leaving as soon as the man, Malik, seemed to think possible...

She clasped her head in her hands, ran her fingers through her hair, trying to stop the panic rattling in her mind.

She needed to take one thing at a time.

She had to go to work this afternoon—did she have something in the freezer for dinner, or should she shop?

This was easier—there was plenty in the freezer, including Nim's other favourite, bolognaise sauce, and she had pasta in the cupboard, but she could make jelly and custard for afters as a treat for Nim.

Nim, who was about to be thrust into a whole new world, far from his friends and all that was familiar to him.

Why was she thinking of jelly and custard when she had Nim's immediate future to consider?

She had a book somewhere—a book Lily had sent when she'd first landed in Madan, which was quite by accident, of course, she'd simply got her flight bookings muddled...

And Nim had looked at the book quite often, though probably not for a year. He knew his father had come from the place in the pictures. They could look at it together—really look from Lauren's point of view—to get some idea of what lay ahead of her, as well as Nim.

She knew from her previous foray on the internet that Madan was an extremely traditional country, still holding onto the past as far as the separation between men and women's roles. Men were heads of the households—the decision-makers—well, she could have guessed that, having met with the strong will of Malik Madani!

No doubt that was what Lily had found difficult, although from the little she'd seen of Tariq and Lily together, Lily had had him wound around her little finger.

Well, she, Lauren, could handle that, and was happy to go about her own business. But the kind of essential part of what lay ahead of her—the marriage deal—was a bit harder to think about.

Although it wouldn't be a real marriage, so maybe she didn't need to think about that part. Malik was an attractive man, and her body was aware of that attraction, but it need go no further—could go no further. It could definitely not become love. She already had one hostage to love in Nim and, given the past, that was more than enough.

It would be a marriage in name only.

And having come full circle in her head, she groaned, stood up and headed for the bathroom. She should have another shower—to clear her head?—then get dressed and go to work. It didn't matter that she'd be early, she could tell whoever needed to be told that she was leaving, then find something to do. Young Eve Lassik rarely had visitors, she could spend some time with her...

But even that plan, feeble though it was, was doomed, for she arrived on the ward to be greeted by Andy, who was duty sister for the day shift.

'Thank heavens you're here,' he said. 'I've just had word from on high that some potential benefactor has arrived and has to be shown around our wards. He's particularly keen to see the new kids' cancer centre and as it's practically your second home, there's no one better to show it to him.'

Should she have felt a premonition of disaster, or a feeling of strange apprehension?

Probably, but she didn't, going blithely to the door of the new unit to meet the representative of the powers-that-be and his or her visitor.

How could she ever have compared Malik to a tailor's dummy? The man walking towards the entrance to the centre seemed to zing with life, his face animated as he spoke to Ross Carstairs, Head of Paediatrics, hands moving with precision through the air as he explained some detail of his conversation.

Was this how Lily had felt when she'd seen Tariq unexpectedly?

Lauren closed her eyes on the thought!

'Ah, Lauren,' Ross greeted her. 'I'm delighted you're here. Andy thought you weren't on until later, but there's

no one better to show Sheikh Madani around the new centre than you.'

Ross turned back to his guest.

'I can leave you in Lauren's capable hands. Lauren, this
is Sheikh Madani. Malik, this is Lauren Macpherson, the
angel of the cancer centre.'

Lauren muttered something she hoped Ross would take
as a welcome to the visitor, while the wretched man looked
down at her and smiled—in delight.

Lauren could see the laughter in his eyes as he said,
'"The Angel of the Cancer Centre", huh? That's some position!'

Lauren turned away from the distraction caused by
laughing eyes.

'This way, please,' she said, brisk and efficient. 'The new
centre has only recently opened. It means we can treat more
children with cancer closer to their homes, which means
less stress on their families. Before it opened, we could do
some treatments, but mainly provided follow-up services
when the children returned from the city hospital.'

'And Susie, was she treated here?'

The question pulled Lauren out of her 'showing the centre' spiel, and she looked directly at the visitor, saw the
smile still lingering in his eyes, felt something flutter inside her, and all but growled at him.

'Are you following me?' she demanded.

And he smiled again.

'*You're* the one not supposed to be here, and I made this
appointment yesterday with your friend Mr Marshall. Well,
he arranged it.'

It was hopeless trying to argue with the man, Lauren
realised, and she should forget about those smiling eyes…

'Yes, Susie was treated here. She was one of our first
patients.'

They'd been walking through the bright lobby, with native birds and animals painted on the walls.

'This is the reception area, as you can see,' Lauren said, in perfect tour-guide mode. 'There are paediatric specialists' rooms at the back on this floor. Most of the city's paediatricians now work out of here.'

She led the way to the elevator.

'The first floor is Day Surgery—and treatment rooms for outpatients. Along here to the left are rooms where children who need intermittent chemo come for treatment, or those who need minor surgery to repair a venous access port.'

'Do you have much trouble with the ports?'

It was an intelligent question, but it was easier to just rattle off information than actually speak to this man she'd said she'd marry.

But she did stop her spiel and turn to him, look at him, as she answered.

'We used to have some trouble with infection, but the new ports, plus more hands-on instruction with the parents or caregivers, has lessened it considerably.'

'Hands-on instruction?'

A serious question, no teasing smile lurking in his eyes, but just looking at him was causing her any number of problems, ninety-nine percent of them physical.

'With new parents—well, parents new to the apparatus—we not only show them what to do and what to look for—slight reddening or a hint of swelling around the port—but we have our own large doll, complete with port, in the children's room so parents can feel the bump beneath the skin. For parents on outlying properties, we have syringes they can use to practise flushing the port themselves, rather than returning here every four weeks so a nurse can do it.'

'And hygiene?'

Lauren shrugged.

'Once the wound has healed where it was inserted, and the dressing removed, it's normal skin care, really. With very young children, we usually keep them overnight after the port's implanted, just to check there are no reactions, but with the older ones, it's day surgery.'

'At home the danger would be infection.'

'Not if the wound is kept dry until it heals,' Lauren emphasised, then his words echoed in her head and she asked, '*Would be* infection? You're not doing it already?'

He sighed.

'I explained our hospital needed money spent on *it*, not hotels. I have made what improvements I can, but for children, particularly those needing chemo, well, I would not allow them to be treated in it. They were sent to a neighbouring country, but now I have a new children's hospital just opened and a dedicated oncology centre within it.'

They were walking on, Malik peering into the different rooms as Lauren spoke.

'Most of the treatment rooms have monitors, so children here for three or four hours while chemo drips into them can watch a variety of television programmes, the older ones have popular computer games they can play and for the younger ones, there are cartoons or simple touch-screen games.'

They took the elevator up, Lauren glad it already had passengers when they entered it, although their presence didn't lessen the physical bombardment his body was causing in hers.

It's a marriage in name only, her head kept telling her, yet the slightest brush of sleeve on sleeve, a hint of his aftershave in the air, could start a flurry of sensations within her, not palpitations exactly, or goose-bumps, but tingling stuff that totally unsettled her...

* * *

'Up here, it's a bit of a free-for-all!' she said, as they left the elevator, but Malik could already see that for himself. The place was a riot of colour, not only the walls with bright murals, but balloons seemed to dance across the ceiling, children's artwork was tacked up everywhere, and a couple of older boys, their mobile drip stands in one hand, were playing football in an open space.

He watched Lauren as she took up her tour-guide spiel again, admiring the sure way she moved, the smiles and sometimes quiet words or gentle touches she gave individual children.

'As you can see, this ward is for older children. Some of them participate in the morning television program they run that is shown throughout the hospital, a few have lessons—we have two teachers—and, generally speaking, it's as homelike as we can make it.'

'It's certainly that,' he said, putting out his foot to kick the straying ball back to the players. 'And younger children?'

'This way,' Lauren said, and Malik followed her again, wondering as he did so why asking her to marry him should have affected him the way it had—as if this would be a normal marriage and his body was already anticipating, well, carnal delights.

He liked the way she moved, this small, determined woman, and as she swept ahead of him, pausing now and then to speak to a patient or staff member, he was seeing her in his new children's hospital, bringing the caring attitude that was obvious with every word she spoke, as well as a wealth of experience.

But thinking this way was folly! Not about the hospital but about attraction. Attraction could lead to love and he was done with that. Romantic love had left him both hurt and humiliated, back when he was young, then seeing the dance Lily had led his brother had put him off the thought of it for ever.

A marriage in name only, that was the idea.

He caught up with her as she paused at one of the hand-wash dispensers, squeezing some foam onto her hands and spreading it thoroughly.

'I'll introduce you to a special friend of mine,' she said. 'Eve has JMML, so bloody rare you wonder why the most vulnerable should end up with it.'

Malik heard the passion of anger in her voice. JMML—juvenile myelomonocytic leukaemia—was very rare indeed. But vulnerable?

Because it attacked children?

Or something else?

Lauren had entered a room so Malik washed his hands and followed to see a small, dark-eyed child with a mop of dark curly hair smiling up at Lauren from her bed.

She was so slight she barely made a bump in the bed-clothes.

'Hi, Evie, I've brought you a visitor,' Lauren was saying quietly. 'His name is Malik.'

The dark eyes turned to study him, then her face changed completely as she smiled. It was as if a light had been lit behind her translucent skin, and he could see the vibrant little girl she'd been before her body had betrayed her.

'Eve's family live a six-hour drive from the hospital, and she has three siblings, so it's difficult for even one of her parents to stay here for any length of time,' Lauren explained.

Explaining vulnerable at the same time—the child alone in a strange city with long separations from her family.

'But I have my phone—see,' the little girl said, reaching out a skeletal arm to lift a phone, with a bright pink case encrusted in sparkling stones, from the table beside her. 'And when I want to talk to them I turn it on and press just here, and at home it comes up on someone's phone or computer and tells them I'm there, and I can do…'

Anxious eyes turned to Lauren.

'What can I do, Lauren?'

Malik saw the fondness for the girl in Lauren's eyes.

'It's called FaceTime, sweetie. Press it to show Malik how quickly your family knows you're waiting to see them.'

Malik watched as the frail fingers manipulated the phone, and within seconds three children's faces appeared on the phone's screen, and excited voices yelled, 'Hello, Evie!'

Malik closed his eyes for an instant and swallowed hard, seeing this sick child connecting with her family so far away.

'How can I help?' he said, aware his voice was rough with the unexpected emotion.

Lauren smiled at him.

'Do you do miracles?' she asked quietly as various people—adults now as well—yelled through the phone to Evie.

He waited.

'The chemo used for AML resulted in a small remission. When she relapsed, she had a splenectomy and again was okay for a while. But now we're waiting for a stem-cell donor. The latest search was hopeful and the donor is being tested now but…'

She was the emotional one now. Malik could hear it in her voice.

'But?' he said, and Lauren shrugged, then visibly brightened.

'Even with the new cells, there's only a fifty percent chance of success, so we're all hanging out for our girl to be in the good half of that statistic.'

'And being positive,' she added, although he sensed she had to try harder for that.

He'd have liked to touch her, rest his hand on her shoulder in a show of support and empathy, but something inside him whispered no, and he looked back at the child who had shut off her phone and appeared to be sleeping.

The tour continued through the rest of the second floor, where there were younger children, play areas with colourful toys, televisions showing children's programmes, the music from them clashing with music from small computers some of the children had.

'It's very special,' he said, already adapting ideas to those that would fit in with his people's culture, his mind ranging ahead to the specialists he'd need for his hospital to become the top children's cancer unit in the region.

And he'd have Lauren—what a bonus! For he understood that this had been four years in the making and in recent years she'd been part of the consulting team when it came to the practicalities of making it a special place. The experience she would bring to his hospital was something he hadn't foreseen when he'd come to find her and Nimr.

And into his head came a vision of the future—he and Lauren working together for the good of his people, his country.

He and Lauren together...

'Thank you,' he said, and meant it in more ways than one, when she finally led him back to the front door. 'I shall see you tonight?' She looked startled.

'I could help you pack,' he offered hopefully, though why seeing her again, as herself and not a nurse, had suddenly become so important he didn't know. Unless the thought of their marriage had sparked an unexpected attraction. Actually, not so unexpected. He'd felt that unfamiliar tug the first time he'd seen her, tired and grubby, her eyes spitting fire at the man who'd organised their meeting.

Whatever, the thought of taking her back to Madan with him was suddenly every bit as important as taking Nimr...

* * *

The question threw Lauren, who was far from convinced this mad idea was real, let alone achievable.

'I'm on duty until ten,' she said. 'Joe's staying in to mind Nim…'

She paused.

'You *could* go to the house,' she said slowly. 'Then you could look at the Madan book with Nim and explain far more about the pictures than I can.'

'You have a book on Madan?"

Lauren nodded.

'Lily sent it when she first went there, and because Nim—well, I thought he needed to know about his father's heritage. He loves it, and looks at the pictures often. He can pick out his father among a group of, to me, anonymous men wearing white gowns. He has a picture of Tariq and Lily and him as a baby, so he knows who to look for.'

'I would enjoy that, and perhaps see you later?'

For some reason the simple question accelerated Lauren's heart rate.

Did he actually *want* to see her?

Or was it for assurance that she hadn't changed her mind?

More likely that, she told herself. This was a practical arrangement after all.

'I'm working until ten, which means it could be midnight before I get home, if there's a problem or a lengthy handover. And believe me, by that time all I want to do is have a quick shower and fall into bed.'

There! That settled any silly heart rate acceleration.

'Of course,' he said politely, further squashing any excitement with his matter-of-fact acceptance of her explanation. 'I shall contact you tomorrow about arrangements.'

She watched him walk away, wondering what on earth she was getting into.

Worse still, wondering why the man was affecting her—no, *attracting* her...

This was to be a business arrangement, not a man-woman thing.

Would the attraction make that harder for her?

Too hard?

She remembered the passion with which Malik spoke of his country, and the things he wished to achieve in order to hand over to Nim a proud country to rule.

And as that was Nim's rightful heritage, would it be fair of her to take it from him?

She glanced at her watch. She could have a quick lunch then see someone in the personnel office to give in her notice.

This time her heart rate slowed—just thinking about such a definitive step made it pause.

'You're doing this for Nim,' she reminded herself, and headed for the canteen.

CHAPTER FIVE

IN THE CABIN of the luxurious private jet the real world seemed far away, far enough away for Lauren to relax. She listened as Malik answered Nim's questions about Madan, and told him stories of Tariq's childhood.

Lauren found herself relaxing, dozing even, until lunch was served, and Nim fell asleep before he'd finished eating.

'He's been so excited about all this,' she told Malik.

He smiled, and said, 'And you?'

'I've barely had time to think, there's been so much to do.'

He smiled again, and said, 'Which I'm certain you managed with great efficiency.'

'Not entirely,' she told him, aware how quickly he could sneak under her defences with a little compliment like that.

To forestall more of them, she added, 'Tell me about Madan.'

And he did, his voice full of pride as he spoke of the past, of passion as he spoke of the future, and of pain when he spoke of Tariq.

She heard truth in his voice as well, and knew, for all her doubts, that this man would never have harmed his brother.

But as they talked—the subjects ranging further now to work, and current affairs, even—she began to feel more and more at ease with him, and sensed he too was relaxing, their togetherness beginning to feel almost natural somehow...

Seen from the air as they came in to land, Madan was an unbelievable landscape of ochre mountains, endless desert, and there, at the top end, the vivid green of the oasis, with towering new buildings clustered around one end of it.

Nim was so excited to be nearing the country of his book he ran from one side of the plane to the other to catch different glimpses of it.

'Time to sit, Nimr,' Malik said, and Nim, already enslaved to this man who'd read his book and talked to him of his father, ran to his seat and buckled his seatbelt.

But as the plane descended, Lauren's misgivings returned, and the questions that haunted her nights—whether she was doing the right thing being the foremost of them—hammered in her head.

Had she spoken aloud? Malik reached over across the aisle and rested his hand on her shoulder.

'Please don't worry, everything will work out for the best.'

Don't worry? she wanted to yell at him.

How could she do that when she was not only stepping into a completely different way of life, language and culture, but in another day or so, according to Malik's well laid-out plan, she'd be a married woman.

And when that simple touch on her shoulder had sent warmth through her skin, how could she do anything but worry? She'd be married in name only, she reminded herself, but somehow that knowledge didn't help to settle the warmth, *or* the turmoil in her stomach, *or* the panicked fluttering of the thoughts inside her head.

They touched down and walked through a crowd of white-robed figures towards a blue and white building, with tall minarets rising from it on all four corners, and a welcoming arched dome painted blue, to mimic the sky, above the entrance door.

Lauren held Nim's hand—probably too tightly—but while he was entranced by all the fairy-tale stuff he saw, she was terrified.

It's just a building, she told herself, *and this is nothing more than another country. People are people everywhere, both good and bad, sick and well. At least work will be familiar...*

'Relax!'

He was by her side, and the word had the sharp note of an order.

But perhaps that's what she'd needed, as she did begin to feel more at ease, smiling as people murmured greetings, releasing Nim so he, too, could he introduced.

Except now the same people she'd smiled at were bowing their heads to Nim as Malik introduced him, and there was something obsequious in the manner of the movement.

Something that unsettled Lauren once again.

'Do they have to do that?' she demanded quietly of Malik as he opened the back of an enormous black car for her.

'Do what?' he asked, his eyes catching hers, arrested by the question.

'Bow and scrape in front of him!' she retorted, angry now. 'We *talked* about it. I told you he should grow up like other boys—' she broke off to tell Nim, who was bouncing on the soft seats to sit still '—not like—oh, I don't know! Someone who should be bowed to!'

Then, exhausted by the strangeness of it all, the travel and her sudden spurt of temper, she slumped into the car beside Nim, pulled on a seatbelt, and tried to calm her breathing.

Go with the flow, she reminded herself, having decided

that was the only thing to do from the day she'd handed in her resignation.

But she hadn't imagined the flow could be interrupted so soon after her arrival.

Or that Malik wasn't travelling with them, for he'd shut the door and the car was sliding silently away from the terminal, through huge golden gates, past the towering hotels, then into the shadows of the mountains she'd seen from the plane, apparently skirting the oases, for on one side of the road was vivid green and on the other the mountains, stark in shadow—*forbidding?*

Lauren shook her head at the fancy in time to turn to see the camels Nim was pointing out so excitedly.

Leaving the mountains behind, they entered an avenue of what Lauren took for date palms, tall and thickly leaved, their fronds almost forming a canopy over the road.

A long road, leading eventually to a high wall, and man squatting outside who stood to open the gates—into a miracle. Before them was the most beautiful garden Lauren had ever seen or imagined, carefully laid out in formal patterns, fountains reflecting a million tiny rainbows.

And roses—everywhere there were roses. There were other shrubs and bushes too, but predominately there were roses in every possible size and colour.

'Gosh, Mum, is this a palace?'

Lauren raised her eyes from the beauty of the garden and saw the magnificence in front of her. Golden domes and minarets, an arched colonnade around the building, sun glinting off the marble of its floor.

Huge wooden doors were, she could see now that she was closer, intricately carved.

'We were supposed to go somewhere else, not to the palace,' she said to the driver, and he must have understood, for he shook his head.

'No palace, no palace,' he said as he alighted and came around to open her door.

A tall, well-built older man, in a black robe trimmed with gold, descended the four steps in a stately manner then bowed to her.

Dear heaven, not the bowing thing again—not to me.

But with Nim he held out his hand, and Nim released his grip on his mother's arm to shake hands with the man.

'Ahmed,' the man said, and Lauren forgot her nerves and stood taller and proud when the four-year-old boy said, 'Nimr,' rolling the final 'r' so beautifully Lauren guessed he'd had some coaching.

Ahmed led the way up the steps, Nim chattering to him about the camels he had seen, unaware he might not be understood.

A young woman, in long loose trousers and a long tunic, stepped out of the shadows of the entrance and came towards them.

'I am Aneesha, I am here to help you.' And with that she took Lauren by one hand and Nim by the other and led them inside. She paused briefly when Nim said, 'Don't forget to take off your sandals, Mum. Remember we read that in the book.'

Lauren had barely taken in the wide entrance hall, with its glorious carpets scattered about the marble floor and hung from many of the walls, when there was a disturbance outside and Malik appeared.

'I am sorry, so sorry. I wished to be here before you but was delayed with some business.'

He'd taken her hand as he spoke, and kept it enclosed in his as he spoke briefly to Aneesha, who nodded to the new arrivals and disappeared on silent feet into the depths of the building.

'Why are we here?' Lauren asked Malik, aware that her hand was responding to his by clinging a bit—well, maybe more than a bit—because somehow holding hands with this man seemed to make everything all right. 'Isn't this the palace?'

He smiled, responding to the movement of her fingers by pulling her a little closer to him, which made her feel even better, though surely that was silly when they barely knew each other.

'This little place? Oh, no, my mother might have insisted on a certain grandeur, but nothing would ever rival the palace, which must be four or five times the size of this humble dwelling.'

'Humble dwelling indeed!' Lauren muttered at him, aware that she should take back her hand but doing nothing. 'And have you been teaching Nim to roll that "r" on the end of his name?'

His only answer was a smile, and as it eased the frightened bits inside her, she also wondered why it had ever made her think of crocodiles.

'Here you will be safe. These people are my people—Tariq's people, too. They will watch over both of you and feel honoured to look after Nimr. But let me show you to your rooms, you must be tired after the journey, then later, perhaps, we can go to the hospital?'

For the first time since he'd burst into her life he sounded a little uncertain as he made that last suggestion.

Almost as if it was important to him that she go, but he was unwilling to push.

Malik uncertain?

She pushed the silly idea away, removed her hand from his and said, 'Then we'd better get going, hadn't we?'

He smiled again, his eyes crinkling at the corners, and for some reason that small, crinkly smile eased a lot of the tension that had been building inside her since the people who were obviously servants had appeared.

But 'rooms' hardly covered the accommodation they

would have, her bedroom lined with silk, hung with drap-
eries, carpets so soft underfoot she was glad she'd left her
shoes outside the front door.

A huge bathroom with a range of luxury products from
bath salts to not-so-humble toothpaste, a dressing room
hung with outfits ranging from jeans—top brands—and
silk shirts to colourful trousers and tunics like the ones the
local women seemed to wear.

'Come and look at my room, Mum!'

Nim came bursting through a door she hadn't noticed,
and she went through it to find a room that would have
filled any small boy with delight.

So much for her hope of bringing him up as a normal
child!

The bed was in the shape of a racing car, spaceships and
satellites hung from a ceiling painted with stars—probably
in their correct astronomical positions, she guessed—while
the shelves held toys and games and large soft animals, particularly tigers in various sizes.

'We don't have tigers living here,' Aneesha was saying
in her soft voice. 'But in the garden the sheikh is running
a breeding programme for the desert leopard, which has
come close to extinction. Would you like to see the baby
cubs?'

Even in his wild excitement, Nim *did* turn to Lauren
for a nod of permission, and although her heart quailed
as her son disappeared through another door into the vast
unknown depths of this enormous building, she had to believe Malik's promise to keep him safe, or she'd go mad
with worry.

'So you trust me?' he said, having come into the room
so quietly she gave a start.

'I *have* to!' she said. 'Who else is there?'

Had she sounded as tense as she felt that he touched her
gently on the shoulder?

'Every person in this building would give his or her life for your son, and you, too, can be sure of their loyalty and protection,' he said quietly, then he drew her unresisting body into his arms and held her against the hardness of his chest, his enclosing arms adding their own promise of security.

And because it was such a relief to have someone else worrying about Nim, she stayed for probably an instant too long, and when he spoke her name she looked up at him, saw something she couldn't read in his eyes, at least until he kissed her.

Just gently, on the lips, a fleeting brush of skin on skin— then he was gone—striding briskly away, pausing at the door to look back at her.

'I will send someone to show you around, or, if you'd prefer to rest, perhaps some tea. I wouldn't leave except there is much to do, and unexpected problems that have arisen in my absence.'

And with that he was gone.

Lauren shook away the silly thoughts chasing through her mind, silly thoughts about that kiss…

It might have come out of nowhere, but it had been re-assurance, that's all it had been.

And though it had caused a myriad of sensations in her body, she could put that down to her unease in this totally new and very, very different situation.

He'd given her a reassuring hug and kiss. What could be more natural?

'Keep telling yourself that,' she muttered, then looked around to check no one could hear her.

She was uncertain what to do. Should she go back to her rooms—her prison?

No way! She was going to have a quick wash, perhaps a coffee if she could find one, then go exploring.

A soft tap at the door was also reassuring. Someone to show her around, perhaps? Offer her tea?

She crossed the vastness of the sitting area and opened the door to find another smiling woman there.

'I am Keema,' the woman said. 'Aneesha, her English better than mine, so she can look after Nimr and teach him our words, and I will look after you.'

Uncertain what to do, Lauren held out her hand.

'I'm Lauren,' she said, and although she'd have liked to add, 'And I can't believe all this is happening,' she thought she might confuse her new friend, so simply ushered her in.

'You would like something before I show you the Sheikh's house?'

'I'd give my—'

And having discarded various things she'd normally have offered to give, like her firstborn—should she ever have one—or her right hand, she went with plain, rather than colloquial, English.

'I'd love a coffee.'

As Keema disappeared, Lauren looked around the room again, discovering her clothes and books had been unpacked and put neatly away in cupboards or on shelves.

Another country, another life…

'Coffee for my lady,' a deep voice said, as once again she chased tremors of trepidation from her mind.

Malik set the small tray on a table in the sitting area, took Lauren's hand again, and led her to a soft couch, settling beside her, which immediately dismissed any remnants of uncertainty.

She'd think why this was so later, but right now he was explaining something.

'I realised I couldn't just walk away and leave you here. It is my job to show you your new home, my job to see that you are comfortable. I have already been away, so affairs of state can wait a little longer.'

He poured the thick black coffee into tiny cups and handed one to her.

'It is not coffee as you know it, and I have that type of coffee should you find this distasteful, but I would like you to try it, if only once.'

A slight smile accompanied the words, and it was that which prompted Lauren to lift the tiny, delicate cup to her lips and take a sip.

Too sweet, was her first thought, and grainy, somehow, but a second sip produced such a feeling of well-being she felt herself relax.

'I could grow used to it,' she said, smiling for the first time since they'd arrived—well, smiling *genuinely.*

'I hope you do,' he said, face serious this time, and she knew behind the words he was telling her he hoped she'd stay.

Because of Nim?

Of course it was!

Their marriage would be one of convenience, which meant she should ignore that tiny spurt of happiness his words had prompted. Ignore the warmth she'd felt when he'd said it, sounding as if he really *did* want her to stay.

Her as well as Nim, perhaps?

But realistically a marriage of convenience would suit both of them, she decided as she took another sip of coffee. They'd both lost loved ones and knew the pain of love...

But as they walked through the vast residence after the coffee he took her hand and tucked it into the crook of his arm, and she began to feel more at ease with this man she didn't know, so by the time he led her along a passage and out into a garden where Nim was playing with two small... kittens? No, these were pale beige little cats with a hint of spots to come. She felt relaxed enough to laugh at the antics of the threesome.

'These are the fourth cub twins we have bred here,' Malik explained to her, before going to kneel by Nim and take one of the cubs gently into his hand.

He lifted the kitten up for her to pat, and as her fingers brushed the silky fur, their fingers met—*eyes* met...

The moment passed, if there was a moment, for now he was speaking to Nim.

'When they are bigger, Nimr, we will take them out into the mountains where they belong, but before that we have to teach them how to look after themselves, so they can hunt for their food in the desert.'

Lauren held her breath, praying Nim wouldn't ask what they ate, but he was already telling Malik the cubs' names and how he could tell one from the other.

'These are better than rabbits, Mum,' he said happily, and Lauren closed her eyes and prayed again, this time that he would have plenty of that happiness in this new life.

'And now I *must* leave you for a while,' Malik said, returning to Lauren's side. 'But I shall return to eat dinner with you and Nimr, and tomorrow, if he is happy to be here with the staff and animals, that is time enough to show you the hospital.'

He put his hand in the small of her back to guide her back indoors, back to her room, where he for stood a moment, looking at her, then touched a finger to her cheek and left.

And, no, she hadn't been waiting for another kiss—or so she told herself...

But she touched her finger to her cheek where his had been, and wondered how things might have been had the two of them met under different circumstances.

It was a foolish thing to think given it was unlikely he'd have even noticed her—and *that* practical thought doused the fluttering flames the touch had left behind.

* * *

Dinner, it appeared, was to be in one of the smaller dining rooms, or so Keema said as she pulled outfits from the wardrobes, holding them up for Lauren's inspection.

Did she have to wear one of them?

Would her own good slacks and a shirt not do?

For a moment she wished Malik was there so she could ask him, then she remembered how disturbed he'd left her feeling and cancelled the idea.

'Look, Mum, I've got a dress!'

Nim burst into the room, in a snowy white, long-sleeved tunic.

'Do you like it?'

Nim nodded.

'I look like the little boys in my book,' he explained. 'I can still wear my other clothes, Aneesha said, but for dinner or going out I wear this.'

He stopped, looking anxious.

'Do *you* like it?'

Lauren smiled at his excitement, although her heart quailed at the speed with which this transformation of her son was happening.

And just her son?

She looked at the outfits Keema had now laid on the bed, and knew she'd have to choose. Her good slacks and a shirt wouldn't cut it at all.

'I'll wear the blue,' she told the young woman, who swiftly removed the other garments.

'That's lovely, Mum.'

Nim stood by the bed, reverently touching the fine material of the dark blue tunic, decorated with silver thread around the neckline and hem.

She slipped into the dressing room to put it on, returning, arms out held for his approval.

'Beautiful!' was the response, only it was Malik there

admiring her, and she could tell from the gleam in his eyes that it *was* admiration—and maybe something else?

'Now we're Madanis,' Nim told her, coming over to take her hand, a little shy, probably because she looked like a stranger.

She certainly felt like one, arrayed in dark blue silk with silver threads. Fairy godmothers and pumpkins came to mind and she smiled to herself.

Malik battled to contain the surge of excitement that had fired his body when he'd seen her.

Marriage in name only?

How could he possibly have thought that would work when something about this woman had attracted him from their first meeting? He remembered the way she'd fired up at the pompous managerial type who'd introduced them, scorn glittering in her eyes!

Now seeing them, the woman and the boy, there in front of him, he knew for certain he had done the right thing. It was personal now. These two were meant to be in his life…

But explaining to Nimr, over dinner, that he was going to marry his mother threw up unexpected difficulties—as far as Nimr was concerned.

'But then you'll be my father,' the little boy said, 'and you can't be my uncle and my father, can you?'

'If that's the worst of his worries, he'll be fine with it,' Lauren said later, when they'd seen Nimr tucked up in bed and were walking in the rose garden.

'He's very accepting of change,' Malik said, 'and I suspect that's your doing. You are his security, and while you are there, he knows everything will be all right.'

'If only it had been that simple for both of us,' Lauren said, and he heard in her voice the fear she'd lived with since the accident.

'It will be now,' he said, slipping an arm around her shoulders and drawing her closer. 'Did I not promise you?'

And as they wandered into the shadows of a rose arbour, he turned her in his arms and kissed her—again a gentle, barely-there brush of lips on lips, only this time, perhaps because the burden of Nim's safety had been lifted from her shoulders, Lauren found herself responding.

Kissing him back, her hands slipping around his chest to keep him close, her lips parting to his questing tongue…

'Marriage in name only?' he said, some time later, as they continued their stroll through the garden. And the teasing quality of his voice sent heat coursing through Lauren's body, until she wondered how they'd tell Nim about the bed-sharing part of what lay ahead, and coldness replaced the heat.

'Marriage in name only!' she said firmly, and hoped she was going in the right direction as she headed back to the house.

'He'll understand—well, maybe not understand but accept,' Malik said, when he'd caught up with her and once again pulled her close, demanding to know what was worrying her.

How could he be so certain, he who'd never had to worry about what lay ahead for a beloved child every minute of every day?

But when he kissed her again, she didn't pull away.

She'd just have to work it out, she decided as she slid into the unexpected delight just kissing this man could bring…

CHAPTER SIX

THE FOLLOWING MORNING, telling herself it was useless to be waiting in her room when she had no idea when Malik might appear, Lauren went out into the back garden, where there were apricot, pomegranate and orange trees, to watch Nim have his first camel ride, then co-opted Keema to give her another tour of the house, this time with local words for each room thrown in.

Walking through it with Malik, she'd counted about ten guest suites like hers, and at least four reception rooms, ranging from ballroom size to a more intimate one that opened onto the colonnade around the house, and would be a pleasant place to entertain.

Dining rooms, too, ranged in size, but one large formal one was set up in what must be a traditional style—no table and chairs but cushions set around a very long mat.

'And the kitchens?' Lauren asked, thinking she might at some stage need to make a snack for Nim.

'Oh, you don't want to go there. There are men—chefs—and they are not family and shouldn't see your face.'

It took a moment for the words to sink in, and when they did register Lauren could only shake her head. Here she'd been, thinking things were not so different from home—except the place was so enormous—then suddenly she was bang up against a local custom.

'But if I wanted to go in?' she asked, and Keema shook her head.

'You must ask for anything you or Nimr need, and we shall bring it to you.'

Lauren thought about arguing—explaining that as an Australian it didn't matter if men saw her face, but Malik appeared from nowhere *and* she completely lost the conversational thread.

And a great deal of composure because one glance at his lips and that second kiss—the one she'd responded to— was front and centre of her mind. Her cheeks turned pink just thinking about it.

'Shall we go to the hospital?' he said. 'I have seen Nimr and explained where I am taking you. He's off to see where the baby camels are kept and be introduced to my birds, so he won't be worried, and Aneesha will see he eats his lunch.'

'And with so many people to take care of my son, I no longer need to be worrying about him?'

Malik smiled.

'I doubt you'd stop no matter how many carers he had or how much assurance I give you.'

She nodded and returned his smile with a small one of her own—small because, while she should feel free to have someone else caring for Nim, she also felt a sudden pang of loss.

Was this how it would be in this new future?

'He will still have time for you,' Malik said, as if he'd read her mind.

And caught something of her feelings, for he put a comforting arm around her shoulders—so much for forgetting about the kiss when just one touch sent her senses spinning—and led her to the car.

It was a smaller car this time—less intimidating but still a sleek and beautiful vehicle.

He drove well, not towards the tall towers of the city but on a road curving back from the mountains and around the outer limits of the oasis to where many squat, brown mud buildings stood, many of them with panels of woven leaves forming parts of the walls, all with intricate balustrading around the roofs, where, from the glimpses of greenery she'd glimpsed, there could be gardens.

'This is how we lived, though the leaders of the tribes always had far bigger places—more like forts than houses. And up ahead, where you see the scaffolding, is my new hospital being built.'

He pulled up on the side of the road so she could see the scaffolding already reaching four or five stories high, and a smaller building at the base of it.

'That's the old hospital—built by the first oil company that came to work our oilfields. It has been adequate for our needs, with a radiology department, pathology department, two operating theatres, with surgeons and trained theatre staff, and many wards.'

'And your staff?'

'They are mainly expats, but we have local doctors who have trained in the UK, including our chief radiologist. Because of having to bring in most of the staff from outside, English is the common language in the hospital. Some of the registered nurses are locals, but most of them aren't, although we have developed an in-hospital training system for enrolled nurses and another one for aides. We also have many aides who work as translators for the expats.'

'I imagine that's important, not to mention easier—having people who can speak to the patients in their own language and carry on proper conversations.'

'You are right, which is why it's important to get our university up and running. I have some friends working on this, but while flashy hotels remain the priority for spending, it is difficult.'

She heard him sigh and wanted to reach over and rest her hand on his thigh, but after last night's kisses, which had left her feeling a bit befuddled, the less she touched him the better.

Had she really responded so readily?

Fiercely might be a better description.

She was considering whether it was a reaction to not having kissed a man for so long, rather than this man in particular, when she realised he was speaking again.

'Many tribal people still use traditional medicine so their doctors have been a wise man or woman in the tribe, who was taught by their predecessor.'

He paused and turned to look at Lauren.

'And I don't know whether it was the outdoor life our ancestors led, or if the traditional medicine worked, but apart from accidents—broken limbs and such—most people lived to a good age.'

'The new hospital—will they come to that?'

'I do hope so, if I ever get it finished. I've been using my own money, but now Nimr is here, I should be able to get government funding for it. But...'

'But?' Lauren echoed, as he started the car again and drove towards the buildings.

'Since the discovery of oil and the wealth that came with it, most of the members of the ruling family and those close to them have been travelling to Europe—England and Germany in particular—for their medical needs.'

'Long way to go to see a GP,' Lauren said, and he smiled.

'Exactly! But that is why my father's generation has never felt the need to spend money on health care here—'

'When *they* had access to it overseas!'

'Exactly!' Malik said. 'Though the first hospital has problems, as you will see, it was still adequate. The oil men left it to the architects who built their hotel, so although they must have looked at plans of hospitals in other places, they didn't see the need for separate facilities and wards for men and women and, more specifically, for children.'

'So?' Lauren asked, guessing there was more.

He paused. Looking into the future?

'So I built the children's hospital first, before starting on the big one. We still use the laboratories in the old hospital—they are in good order—but eventually those in the new building will cover both and the old building can be demolished.'

He'd pulled up at the side of the old building and led the way inside.

'This was originally a grand entrance foyer, like the hotels have, then behind it, to one side, was—well, still is—the reception desk, and on the other side the emergency department. Unfortunately, many people saw this big space as ideal for a market—somewhere to sell their wares to patients and their families or other visitors. So now we use a side entrance for the ED and the main hospital, although some people still try to get in through this maze.

Lauren looked around. Fans whirred overhead and people milled around the great space, bargaining, shouting, chattering—so much noise and confusion.

'There's a man selling pomegranates over there!' Lauren said, indicating the man with a nod of her head.

'That's nothing,' Malik said gloomily. 'We had a patient from Pakistan in here once—many of the oilfield workers are expats—and his visitor was a snake charmer, complete with snake. The problem is, our people are not used to the hospital concept. They are family-oriented, so they want to be close to the patient. Ideally, they would like to stay with the patient in the ward or room, and if they can't they are likely to camp close by, so the market does a thriving business.'

'And in your new hospital? Will it be different?' Lauren asked.

He smiled at her.

'I hope so! My idea is that when it is completed, the old one can be turned into a kind of hotel, where families of the patients can stay free of charge.'

'And the market?' she asked, still enthralled by the madness of it.

'Will probably remain,' he said, so gloomily she had to laugh.

'It's not funny,' he told her sternly, but she caught the twinkle in his eyes, and laughed some more.

He led her around to the side entrance, but the tour was perfunctory, little more than hand-waving in one direction or another, rooms and wards labelled but not investigated.

'You'll see it all eventually,' he said as they came out through another side door at the other end of the market, 'but if you decide you want to work, it will be with the children. So now I'll show you my children's hospital.'

And the pride in his voice was enough to tell her it would be very special.

They walked around to the side of the new building where a gleaming white structure stood.

Lauren had to blink and look again but, no, her first impression had been right. It looked like a castle from a fairy story, with a big golden dome and tall, slender spires decorated with pink and blue—even what looked like a fort built at one side.

'It's a hospital?' she asked, unable to hide the wonderment in her voice.

Malik paused and turned towards her, guiding her into the shade of a tree where they could talk and see the incredible building.

'We had a sister, Tariq and I, who was very ill from the time she was born. I was too young to know details of her illness, and neither my mother nor my father ever spoke of it, so even later, when I began to study, I couldn't really work out what it had been.'

'She died?' Lauren asked, and he nodded.

'But for many years she was in and out of the hospital—which was new then. She was even flown overseas to see specialists. And one time when she was home and we were playing by her bed, and talking with her, she told us how horrible hospitals always looked and asked if they had to look like that.'

'Poor kid!' Lauren said, giving in to the need to touch his arm.

He smiled at her, laid his hand over hers, and continued, 'So we asked her what a children's hospital should look like. Tariq was good at drawing and he found paper and coloured pencils and she told him what to draw.'

'And this is *it*?' Lauren asked, shaking her head in disbelief that this magic castle could possibly be a hospital.

Malik smiled.

'It is my memorial to a brave little girl,' he said, his voice deep with emotion. 'The original drawing is framed on a wall inside, and we didn't put it on a mountain-top, as she'd have liked—that was a bit too inconvenient.'

He smiled again, apparently delighted at her reaction.

'Come, I'll show you around,' he said. 'It's spread out because with children it really *had* to be ground floor so the families from out of town can camp close by, so it sometimes seems, at the end of the day, that you've walked many miles.'

Was he talking too much because he was worried she might not like his ambitious project?

But as he led her through the doors and she saw the bright painting of a camel train threading its way around the walls, she couldn't stop smiling, her face radiating delight as she turned to him.

'It's fabulous!' she said, and it took a great deal of will-power to remain all business in the face of her delight. What he'd really have liked to do was take her hand and walk around the walls with her, explaining the intricately woven camel bags hung on the camels and telling her stories of the past.

Just to see that smile again?

Of course.

But also just to be with her as man and woman without all the complications in his life and those he'd forced into hers. To see her smile, and feel the heat inside him that a simple smile could generate—to see where the attraction he knew was between them could lead...

'And this is just the entry,' he told her. 'Emergency is through this way.'

They entered, and he was barely through the door when someone called to him.

'Dr Madani!'

It was a nurse he knew and trusted, so he headed to the cubicle to see a small boy, about two, lying on the bed.

'A seed of some kind up his left nostril. I don't want to try to dislodge with the crocodile clips, in case I push it further in.'

She handed him the otoscope, which was used for both nose and ears, and, after greeting the anxious mother beside the bed with a smile and a brief chat with the small patient, he bent over to have a look.

Such a young child—they could really only do it under anaesthetic, and he avoided anaesthetising children whenever possible.

'Do you know the trick that sometimes works?' Lauren said. 'I saw a doctor do it once and have used it many times since.'

He smiled at her—he might have known she'd come up

with something, for he was beginning to realise that this woman was special in every way.

And his heart was smiling, too, as if this very ordinary conversation was a personal confirmation of the rightness of their match...

'Do tell,' he said, and she explained how she could block the free nostril while the mother blew hard into the child's mouth.

'You'll have to translate and tell her it might not work, but it's worth a try before anaesthetic.'

He explained to the woman, who was reluctant at first, but now Lauren was at the child's level, stroking his arm and playing with his fingers, the mother agreed.

And as Lauren pressed the free nostril shut and the mother blew, the seed *did* come out, to the delight of all.

'I can't have spent enough time in emergency rooms to have learnt that trick,' Malik said, when mother and son had departed.

'It's an old one and a good one, so now you know,' Lauren told him, her smile again causing a response in his heart.

He showed Lauren around the wards, which were sparsely occupied.

'Parents are wary about coming to the hospital in case they discover their child will have to stay, even for a short time. It is not their way, but they will learn in time. Attendance in Emergency is doubling every month, and we have arrangements so at least two people—usually the mother and grandmother, or an aunt—can be with any child in the wards at all times.'

He was leading the way into a wing off the main foyer, nodding and greeting staff as they passed.

'It's not big enough yet to have designated post-op or

ICU wards, but these rooms are set aside for those purposes.'

He knocked and opened a door into a small, bright room, the two women in it adjusting their head scarves to cover all but their eyes but nodding to him, their eyes telling Lauren they were both smiling, too.

The patient lay on his back—a small boy about Nim's age, she guessed. His right foot and lower leg were in a cast and suspended in a cradle above the bed.

Broken ankle? she wondered, watching Malik as he tickled the boy's toes to make them wiggle, talking quietly to him at the same time, before turning to speak to the women, presumably about the child's treatment.

Although the conversation was going on for some time, now it must be about her, for both women were nodding and smiling in her direction.

Lauren smiled back and waved to the little boy, who hid his face behind his hands, then waggled a couple of fingers at her as Malik ushered her out of the room.

'I was telling them you are a children's nurse,' Malik explained. 'Abu, our patient, was born with a club foot and although that would have been something he could live with in another age, we now have proper facilities and a paediatric surgeon who will fly in when necessary.'

'Did gentle stretching and a cast soon after birth not help?' Lauren asked, as she'd assisted in such manoeuvres herself.

Malik shook his head.

'We didn't meet Abu until a fortnight ago, when someone persuaded his mother to bring him here. The foot was badly deformed by then because of the way he'd been walking on it and was causing him a lot of pain.'

'Poor kid, but at least they *did* come, and it won't be something he has to put up with for the rest of his life.'

They'd reached an open area, where beds could be separated by curtains. Two young girls in pyjamas, one with a tiara on her head, were playing on the floor in one corner, an array of toys around them.

'I've been told this open ward is a mistake for Madan, but children enjoy the company of other children, and I believe that as parents get used to the idea of hospitals, there will be less insistence on being present at all times. Most of the children we've had in here are children of expats working here, and if it is a local child then you'll see the curtains drawn around the bed most of the day and night.'

'Because the women visitors can't be seen by men who aren't related?'

Malik nodded, then shook his head.

'Not that many of the men come to visit—fathers sometimes do but generally it is felt that children's illness is women's business.'

'Things aren't that much different at home,' Lauren told him. 'The fathers come because they love their children, but some of them find it very difficult to see their child sick or hurting.'

Malik nodded.

'Already I would feel that with Nimr,' he said, sounding as if the thought had surprised him.

They walked through two more wards, meeting nurses and doctors on the way and stopping to speak to children so Lauren could get some idea of the patients she would have.

'And this is Graeme Stewart,' Malik said, pausing in front of an older man. 'I trained under Graeme in London and as he is now semi-retired, he kindly agreed to hold the fort here for me while I sort out the family business.'

Lauren smiled at the man, enjoying the still distinctive Scottish burr beneath his English voice.

'You might be coming to work here?" he asked, and Lauren nodded.

'As soon as I know my son is settled in and happy with his carers,' Lauren told him.

'I will look forward to it. I would like to see more training going on with the young enrolled nurses, and you would be a great help there.'

The flutter of excitement Lauren felt at getting back to work—of having something normal in her life—must have shown on her face, for Malik said, 'You love it, don't you? Nursing?'

She nodded, unable to deny it, knowing how much she'd missed it in the two years she'd spent running with baby Nim.

'He will be safe if you wish to start immediately,' Malik said. 'And he seems happy outside, playing with the animals.'

'He is,' Lauren replied, although inside she knew she wanted more for him—some other children to join the play so he had the socialisation he'd had at kindy.

Not that she'd worry Malik with that now, when he obviously had problems of his own.

'And you?' Malik asked. 'Are you feeling settled?'

Lauren laughed.

'Hardly,' she told him. 'We've been here barely twenty-four hours, but I think when I go back to work, it will seem more normal.'

Best not to mention that any unsettled feeling she was having was to do with him more than his country.

'That is good,' he told her, 'for there is something I must explain. I spoke of our marrying within days of arriving here, but there are problems within our council of elders that must be sorted out. A question of the succession...'

He spoke so gruffly she knew the problems must be worrying him. Succession?

Wasn't she here to ensure he would have the position of regent to Nim?

Wasn't that the succession?

Should she ask him about it?

She shook away the thought. She might not have been here long, but she'd picked up some of the cultural differences in the lines drawn between men and women. If he wanted her to know, surely he would tell her...

'You must do what you have to do,' she told him, resting her hand on his shoulder. 'With the helpers you have given us, Nim and I will be fine.'

He nodded and touched her hand where it still lay on his shoulder—a thank-you kind of touch, she knew, for all it sent a cascade of shivers down her spine.

'I'll drop you home,' Malik said quietly, and although the word evoked images of the home she'd had and the life she'd led, she knew, given time, she could get used to their new 'home'. Especially once she went back to work and life began to feel normal...

Malik literally dropped Lauren at the house, feeling bad that he did no more than open the car door for her and kiss her lightly on the cheek, before heading back to the council chambers in the palace where things were in such turmoil he wondered if he really wanted the job of sorting it all out.

But apart from it being the right thing to do—taking Lauren to the hospital—he'd also *wanted* to.

Wanted to spend a little time in her calming presence, to feel her close to him, smell the lingering scent of roses in her hair.

He groaned to himself, aware there'd be less turmoil in the council if he went along with marrying a Madani woman, aware also, if he pushed through his marriage to Lauren, the decision could make life here difficult for her.

And that was the last thing he wanted, for the more he saw of her, the more he respected and admired her—loved her, even?

No way! It was attraction he was feeling, and her response to his kiss the previous evening suggested it wasn't all one-sided.

But love?

It was a concept that sat uncomfortably in his mind, for love—apart from his love for Tariq and their younger sister—hadn't featured much in his life.

Besides which, he'd lost both of them—both the people he'd loved.

Would he risk it again?

He shook his head, more to shake away the thoughts than to answer an unanswerable question.

So, back to the endless arguments, *and* back to his search through the palace occupants for the person who had killed his brother, because while that person was alive and still plotting, Nimr could be in danger.

He drew up at the palace, aware that the place where he'd grown up had changed.

Or had his own suspicion charged the atmosphere around him?

The day dragged on, with arguments and counter-arguments, the council breaking into small discussion groups—talking, talking, talking, something his people loved to do.

And all he could think about was getting back to his mother's house in time to sit with Nimr while he had his dinner, read him a bedtime story, then maybe persuade Lauren to dine with him, to spend some time alone with her, walk in the rose garden, perhaps.

Excitement stirred, and he forced his mind back to whatever discussion was currently raging around him.

'Is there trouble?' Lauren asked, seeing the lines of tiredness in Malik's face.

'I will sort it,' he said, but Lauren knew when they'd

sat with Nim while he'd had dinner, then read the bedtime story together, that something had been worrying Malik.

Would he tell her?

Let her share the burden?

It was what she wanted if they were to have a real relationship—a sharing of concerns as well as joys.

And just where had the idea of a 'real' relationship come from? A few touches? A kiss?

But as she asked herself the question, she knew, for whatever reason, that was what she wanted.

'I will handle it,' he said again when she asked over dinner. 'Let's talk about Nimr. Who are these friends he spoke of?'

So he wasn't going to share, but that was okay—they were still virtual strangers, really.

Added to which, this was a very different culture from her own, and even in the short time she'd been here, she had become very aware of that.

She changed the subject, talking about Nim, hoping some general chat might help him relax.

'Keema's sister has two boys, one a year older than Nim and one a year younger. The sister brought them over to play and Nim just loved having the company, although he's turning into a show-off, acting as though the leopard cubs, and camels, and even your falcons are his.'

'Boys have their own way of levelling things out,' Malik said, smiling at some memory of his own. 'But that is good. He needs some friends and I know Keema's family.'

'Is that important?' Lauren asked. 'Will you always have to be aware of who his friends are? Is it because you think he's still in danger?'

And if Malik had looked weary when she'd first seen him, he looked exhausted now.

'My instinct—no, my belief—is that no one would openly attack a member of the royal family here in Madan.

We are too revered by the people. There would be public outrage, and that is why I wanted you here, not in Australia. But until I find who harmed his father, I cannot take any chances,' he said, anger twisting through the tiredness in his voice.

Lauren waited, knowing there was more—wishing she could do something, help him in some way.

'So, until I *do* find the person behind Tariq's death, Nimr will be guarded, not by soldiers with rifles but by people who will shadow him at all times. Ordinary people in appearance—unobtrusive, but still there.'

He turned to her with a tired smile.

'Did I not promise you that?'

He sounded so stressed she was sorry she'd brought it up, so she stood up and held out her hand.

'Let's walk in the garden—forget all the bad stuff and just enjoy the peace and beauty.'

They walked in silence, arm in arm, Lauren happy to be with him, this man she was getting to know. She'd seen him as a caring professional at the hospital, had watched his gentle interaction as he eased himself into Nim's life, and read his tortured soul when he'd spoken of his brother and of the plight of his people as they entered a new age.

But as they walked the scented paths, she felt him relaxing, and when they kissed in the shadowy colonnade she knew he wasn't thinking of his country's problems, or of revenge, for his body told her of his need for physical comfort—something that had been missing from her life too in recent years.

'We are not married yet, but I *will* marry you—even if it means leaving my country to live in yours, or anywhere you choose.'

He'd interrupted her in mid-kiss so it took her a few seconds to catch on to what he was actually saying.

She drew back far enough to see his face, although their

arms still linked their bodies. And although it had shaken her, she'd leave the last bit of his explanation for another time. Right now, tired and worried as he was, he needed reassurance, and something inside her wanted to give it to him.

'I don't need a promise of marriage from you to take this further, Malik. We're both adult enough to admit there's an attraction between us—our kisses have proved that— so what's to stop us finding pleasure in each other without strings, or ties, or any thought for the future?'

He kissed her again, so deeply and thoroughly Lauren felt herself melting, sagging against his body as her body demanded more.

Lifting her effortlessly into his arms, he strode with her along the colonnade and in through filmy curtains to a room in one of the smaller suites.

A lamp glowed faintly beside a massive bed that enveloped them both as he set her down and lay with her, kissing, murmuring words she didn't understand, hands learning her body as hers learned his.

But for all they'd slowed their pace, in the end desire took control and it was a frantic coupling, both of them half-dressed, until they lay exhausted, still entwined, their bodies exchanging silent messages where skin met skin, or pulse met pulse.

'This is *not* how it should have been!' Malik muttered, what seemed like a long time later but was probably just as soon as he could breathe normally enough to speak.

'You didn't enjoy it?' Lauren teased, and he took her in his arms, turning her to lie on top of him, holding her close.

'More than I could ever say,' he murmured against her neck. 'But I must go, and Nimr will want to find you in your own bed in the morning. Shall we walk together before we part?'

It was more than a question, yet not quite entreaty. This man, she knew for certain, would never beg.

But she understood he needed her to walk with him, to normalise things once again.

'Of course,' she teased. 'However would I find my bedroom if I don't come in the front door and count the rooms I pass until I come to mine?'

He laughed and held her closer.

'You are special,' he said, and the unexpectedness of the words—not a declaration of love or even desire—warmed her body in a way she'd never felt before.

An everyday word, but it drove deep into her heart and banished the bits of uncertainty his earlier words had left behind.

And much as she longed to know what was going on in his world, she knew he was a man brought up to protect the womenfolk in his life from trouble and concerns.

Sharing these with a woman would be totally alien to him, which didn't stop her hoping that one day he might.

Malik drove back to the palace where he was staying until they could marry. Back to the discord and scheming and some people's determination he should not marry Lauren.

He'd kind of let that slip tonight when he'd spoken of marriage, but doubted she'd picked up on it. He hoped she hadn't as he didn't want to worry her. She'd already carried fear as her shadow for four years—did she not deserve some peace and security?

And how could he explain the council of elders to a newcomer anyway? Explain that while he might eventually be regent and head of the country until Nimr came of age, the elders acted more like a Western parliament with the right to make laws.

In this case a particularly divisive and inexplicable law.

But could he leave his country?

Betray his people by leaving when they needed him most?

He knew he couldn't—wouldn't—for all it would be the easiest of solutions.

So he'd have to fight, and after tonight, and a taste of what could be between Lauren and himself, how could he not?

CHAPTER SEVEN

THE MEASLES EPIDEMIC struck swiftly and viciously, five children presenting at the hospital with a rash giving warning of what was to come.

'Five in one day—how bad *is* it out there?' Malik growled at Lauren, who'd come in answer to an urgent summons, leaving Aneesha and Keema to entertain Nim.

'Has no one been vaccinated?' she asked, and saw him shake his head gloomily.

And much as she'd have loved to touch him on the arm, to offer comfort of some kind, they were at the hospital, there were people everywhere, and a touch was out of the question.

Which was probably just as well, considering how his touches distracted her.

'I did set up a vaccination programme when I first returned from my specialty four years ago, fired up with enthusiasm to save the children of my country. But my father was ailing and the elders didn't push it. I should have overseen it but, with Tariq missing and then dead, and the new hospital being built, it was all I could do to keep working at my job, let alone think of other things.'

'And the hospital staff?'

'At least they have all had every vaccination and inoculation available.'

'That's great! Can we get a good supply MMR vaccine flown in?' Lauren asked. 'If we can get enough from outside sources, we can start vaccinating now, children first, then the adults because it won't spare anyone. School children we can do at school.'

Offering practical help was better than touching, but he paled and said, 'Nimr, he's vaccinated?'

He really, really needed that touch.

She made do with a nod.

'Me too, and you should have been before you worked in a hospital. What about palace staff? The staff at your mother's house?'

'I did them myself, back when I started it.'

'So some of them can help by going out and convincing people to come. Have we staff enough to cover the actual vaccinations?'

Malik had to smile at the passion in this woman, who had leapt on the problem like a—well, tiger—and was following thought alleys he hadn't even considered.

And much as he'd have liked to drag her into the nearest broom cupboard for a quick kiss—or just a hug—he ignored the physical sensations that being near her always brought, and went with practical instead.

'I will get whatever we need. Some vaccine is on the way, but you are right. Using the media to tell people to come will not be enough, we need women talking to other women. Adults who contract it can be at more risk of complications than children.'

'And maybe we can designate a space in a ward for the vaccinations or—'

She stopped and looked up at him.

'Would they come to your mother's place? We could do it in the garden—in the colonnade—so the children could play outside while parents waited in line.'

'And we'd be keeping them well away from the hospital where the infection could easily be spread.'

He smiled at her, so aware of her it was a wonder she couldn't feel the heat.

'It will be an added incentive—visiting a big house and a garden. All people are curious.'

And Lauren, when she had time to think about it, had been amazed at just how quickly her idea turned into reality. Refrigerators were set up to hold the vaccine, experienced nurses brought in to administer it, house staff set to keeping order in the queues while others went out to markets and meeting places to hand out information and talk to families, both offering vaccinations for the well and explaining how to care for the sick, with plenty of fluids and bed rest until the rash began to disappear.

But that was happening in a different world, for at the hospital both children and adults with serious complications had been admitted, and the staff, Lauren included, were run off their feet caring for the influx of patients.

She saw Malik most days, though often he was there when she was snatching some sleep in the nurses' quarters at the back of the building while he took on the night duty. At least Nim was safe and happy, and over the last two years had become used to her odd hours. Sometimes, when she'd been on duty at home—especially on split shifts— she'd caught only glimpses of him for a few days, but had made it up to him on her days off.

Graeme was a constant daytime presence on the wards, dispensing both drugs and advice. The most common problems were flu-like symptoms and high fevers, although many of the children also suffered from sore eyes.

Their most complicated case was a young girl who'd had seizures brought on by her fever, and though she was stabilised, she was listless and pale—uncomplaining but far from well.

'Let's take some blood, there has to be something else going on,' Malik suggested, on a rare day he'd appeared on the ward while she was there.

And simply standing beside him as they looked at the child was enough to keep Lauren going.

'Encephalitis,' she said, remembering a list she'd read of possible complications. About one in a hundred children could contract pneumonia and one in a thousand encephalitis. 'Can we do a spinal tap for some cerebrospinal fluid?'

Malik nodded.

'I'll speak to her parents, get a brain scan too, to check for swelling, not that there is much we can do—although anti-viral medicines and immuno-suppressants might help.'

He moved towards the door of the darkened room, the blinds drawn to protect the child's eyes, then turned back to Lauren, who was checking on the bag that dripped fluid into the sick girl.

'I don't know how I would cope if it was Nimr,' he said, and the gruffness in his voice told Lauren just how deeply his feelings were for his new-found nephew.

'Nim will be fine,' she told him, keeping the arms she wanted to put around him firmly by her side. 'So let's get these other kids better.'

But as more people were answering repeated radio and television broadcasts to be vaccinated, the situation at the house became overwhelming. More vaccine was flown in, and Lauren, aware the children's hospital was managing— just—turned her attention to vaccination.

With Aneesha beside her to translate when necessary, she joined the nurses at the house, reforming the system so they had three orderly queues—women with children, men with children and adults on their own.

'In a story, romance could blossom in the adults' queue,'

she said to Aneesha as they took a break on the edge of the fountain, eating watermelon from a tray, replenished often and left on a bed of ice, for everyone to help themselves.

'Is it my imagination of are there more children here than earlier?' she asked, and Aneesha smiled.

'Those at school come when it finishes at one o'clock. They want to play with Nimr in the garden.'

'Girls and boys?' Lauren asked as she peered at the children dancing along the garden paths, seeking the head of one she knew.

Aneesha smiled.

'At this age they are just children and it is good for them to play together. Your Nimr is a leader, see him there...' She pointed to the far corner where some kind of fort seemed to have appeared. 'He organised that old building into a pretend castle—I think a castle, although sometimes it is a spaceship. While I am with you, Keema watches from afar, while other staff are always nearby.'

Lauren closed her eyes, thinking how little she knew of her son's life these days. They still had their morning cuddles when he filled her in on what he'd been up to and most days she was home from work in time to sit with him at dinner—Malik joining them when he could—but it had been a shift in the level of their togetherness.

Her baby was growing up...

And perhaps that was a good thing, she decided as she faced the world again, finishing her watermelon and turning to wash her hands in the clear waters of the fountain.

As dusk fell, the queues didn't seem to have diminished.

'You've done enough,' she told Aneesha. 'Have a break, I'll manage, but when you're ready, would you round up Nim and get him fed and into bed?'

'I shall not have to round him up, as you say,' Aneesha told her, 'for here he is.'

Two equally grubby boys had appeared from the garden, Nim beaming as he led his new, and apparently very shy, friend towards Lauren.

'Mum, this is my friend Najeeb, and he's four but he goes to school. Can I go to school too—please, Mum, please.'

His eyes were big with entreaty—this member of the ruling family wasn't afraid to beg.

'I'll find out about it,' she promised him. 'But now you're too dirty to be here where people are having their injections, so around the back with you. Aneesha will give you a bath and your dinner. I'll be in to say goodnight but these people need me right now.'

'That's okay, Mum. Najeeb's little sister is sick, and I know you're trying to stop other people getting it. Najeeb had his injection yesterday, that's when I met him.'

'And his mother or father? Who is with him?'

'His big sister. She's still in the queue.'

'Then let us find her,' Aneesha said. 'I will tell her I'll take you both for a bath and where she can come to eat with us.'

'Maybe find her and send her to me,' Lauren said. 'A little queue-jumping doesn't hurt once in a while, and I wouldn't want her becoming anxious for her brother.'

But the sister, when produced, was far from worried.

'I speak good English so I can help while Aneesha takes the boys,' she said. 'I want to be a nurse, and when I finish school I hope to start at the hospital for some training.'

Aware that many of the nurses she'd met had been abroad for training, Lauren, in between patients, asked if that had been an option.

She shook her head.

'My father left and my mother has died. I must care for Najeeb until he comes of age.'

Lauren nodded. These things happened everywhere, she knew, but her heart ached for the girl who'd taken on such a burden.

By ten that night, they'd cleared the palace grounds of people wanting vaccinations and those who, Lauren suspected, simply came to look around. The girl and Najeeb had both been fed and sent home in a car, and as the servants cleaned up the debris of the day, Lauren took herself wearily to her rooms to shower and clamber into bed, ignoring the plate of pastries Keema brought for her, and the coffee, although she had to admit it had kept her going through the day.

The following day was not as bad, and two days later they could shut the gates, anyone still wanting vaccination told to report to the hospital.

Lauren was up and aware that she, too, should be heading to the hospital, *wanting* to be heading to the hospital, if only to see Malik.

Silly, really, how much she'd been missing him—how much her body had been missing him—and this after just one brief sexual encounter, a kiss or two, and touches that sent fire along her nerves.

She should be thinking about Nim, not Malik.

He was fixated on the school idea, and although she knew she'd have to discuss it with Malik, Lauren decided she could at least take a look.

'Is it far?' she asked Aneesha, who had offered her services again as translator, while Keema played with Nim.

'Not far,' was the reply, so they set out on foot, walking for what seemed like miles to Lauren, with the sun growing perceptibly hotter as they went.

'I thought you said not far,' she complained to Aneesha. 'I thought that meant it was just around the corner. We should have brought water—no, we should have called a car.'

She knew she sounded cross and apologised, trudging on in the oppressive heat.

Malik picked them up as Lauren was certain she was

about to die in the dry, desert heat, helping her into the soft leather seat in the front, where the air-conditioning washed around her like a cold shower.

'Why didn't you call for a car?' he demanded crossly. 'Only total idiots walk around in this heat! And where the hell did you think you were going?'

Lauren breathed in a little more cool air before answering.

'To a school, to check it out for Nim, but I think it will be too far for him to walk at his age, and I was only going to look, so I could talk to you about it.'

He'd handed her a bottle of cold water, and she stopped her explanations to drink thirstily.

'He has wanted to go to school for so long and it will be better for him to be with other children, instead of hanging around being spoilt by the servants.'

And having explained this, Lauren lay back in the, oh, so comfortable seat, then turned to check that Aneesha was still with her and had some water.

But Malik had also turned to Aneesha, who was now answering his questions.

'Forget that school, there are better ones, and I will sort one out for Nimr. Right now, I'll take you home,' he muttered to Lauren when the conversation finished. In spite of Aneesha's explanations, or perhaps because of them, he was still obviously angry.

'But his friend is at that school, we should at least look at it,' Lauren argued.

'Not when you're exhausted. Walking in the sun was madness, especially when you need to rest. You've been working practically non-stop for days, and I can't be there right now to keep an eye on you—there is just too much going on. I'll drive you straight home!'

Lauren straightened in her seat, fastened her seatbelt

and said, *'After* we've seen the school. Nim is *my* child and I don't need you "sorting" his school!'

She was aware they shouldn't be having this argument in front of Aneesha but right now she was too tired to care.

'Anyway,' she continued, giving him no time for another objection, 'this is so much better, seeing it together. We'll be able to discuss it properly.'

Malik spoke to Aneesha again and with a sound that just might have been his teeth grinding took off along the road they'd been following.

The school was everything Lauren could have hoped for—a mix of local and expat children, most lessons in the native language, although English was also taught.

'He won't understand his lessons,' Malik grumbled.

'He's four—they're hardly doing algebra. It's more play learning, socialising, interaction with each other at that age. These things are important, Malik. Important to him, and important to me.'

To her astonishment, he looked at her and smiled, his anger gone.

Because she'd said it was important to her?

And although she could see he was exhausted, the smile he gave her as he agreed was warm enough to lift her spirits, to the extent that when they returned to the house she suggested they drop Aneesha off.

'I'll come back to the hospital with you. There'll be something I can do.'

He hesitated, then shook his head.

'I suppose if I don't take you, you'll set off on foot again.'

Lauren laughed.

'Oh, no, that's one lesson I *have* learned. I won't walk anywhere on these hot days.'

And just like that camaraderie between them returned, and beneath it, even in their less than upbeat state, hummed the attraction...

CHAPTER EIGHT

NEW CASES OF measles continued to come in to the hospital, the vaccinations taking time to work, and the airborne virus seemingly able to strike at will. But now Nim was going happily off to school each day, being at work where she was needed was a kind of antidote to this new stage of his life.

'Keema tells me there's a huge market not far from the hotels,' Lauren said, catching up with Malik in the hospital where she was still spending most mornings.

He'd looked surprised to see her, yet his tired face had softened into a smile.

'So?'

'I'm thinking those people might not have access to radio or television and aren't aware of the risks in crowds of people. Can we close it?' she asked.

'That market is the hub of the city. Closing it would be unthinkable.'

'So more people will get sick,' Lauren said. 'How fair is that? And look at you—when did you last sleep? You can't go on like this, you'll be ill yourself. I know the hospital is still coping with all the usual cases as well as the measles outbreak, but you need a break.'

His smile grew wider, glinting in his eyes.

'And is this the nagging wife I'll have if we marry?" he teased, and she laughed, that glint in his eyes bringing her body to life with the usual rush of sensations just being near him could produce.

'I'll be far worse than this!' she told him. 'Now go and rest!'

But as he walked away she added, 'And close the market!'

But later, back in the children's hospital where the little girl had had the diagnosis of encephalitis confirmed, she paused by the child's bed, checking the fluid bag, the cannula, reading through the chart and thinking, in another corner of her mind, about the word Malik had dropped into their earlier conversation.

That tiny but, oh, so powerful word: *if*...

He's tired, it just sounded wrong, she assured herself, but still it jangled.

Was it a warning bell?

Maybe, but why was it worrying her? She hadn't been keen on the marriage idea from the start—*and* had told Malik he needn't promise marriage to act on their shared attraction.

So why worry now over one little *if*?

Because you're falling for him, that's why, she told herself. *The attraction was there from that first meeting, you know that, and in your head you've really grown to like the idea of marrying him...*

The medical situation eventually eased, although Malik was caught up with ensuring a regular vaccination program was set up, covering all the preventable diseases.

He'd call in at dinnertime to say hello to Nim, but as many of the people he had to speak to were in different time zones, he rarely stayed.

'I need vaccines but also places to store them safely,' he said to Lauren, when they met in the staffroom at the children's hospital one morning. 'And staff to look after

the storage facilities as well as trained staff to administer the drugs.'

'And no doubt another level of administrators at the
top, to work out programmes and see they are carried out.'

He nodded grimly.

'Not to mention a committee of community leaders to
advise people to take up the service for their own, and their
children's, safety.

'All the things a health department does,' Lauren teased,
and he agreed.

'We have gone past the time when a group of elders
could handle all aspects of our people's private lives. We
need to find some form of government acceptable to our
people. Up until now, we've had the elders each tasked with
a different job—one overlooking road construction, one
liaising with the oil people, another in charge of schools,
health and welfare, and so on. But with the nation growing
at an unprecedented rate, these things must be formalised,
and administrations put in place.'

'And you're the one who has to do it? Organise all this?'

She'd made coffee and found honey cake as he talked,
and now she poured him a cup and eased him into a chair.

'Here, forget it all for a few minutes, just relax.'

She set the coffee beside him on a small table, and as
she turned to get the cake, he caught her hand, held it, the
look on his face telling her he had needed that touch as
much as she had.

'I could not have done this without you,' he said, and,
embarrassed at the rush of feeling she'd experienced, she
laughed.

'Of course you could. You might have ended up even
more tired than you are, though I doubt that's possible,
but I've done nothing more than any nurse would do. And
we've got through it, haven't we?'

She eased her hand from his for all she'd have liked to

leave it there—warm and safe. 'And as for all this admin stuff, that will get done in time—it doesn't need to be done tomorrow, you know.'

He looked at her now, shadows in his dark eyes.

Was it tiredness?

Or something else?

She had no idea, but she had to drink her coffee and leave this room before she sat down on his knee and put her arms around him and told him everything would be all right.

Even though, since that little 'if' had entered her life she wasn't sure it would be.

And now it was at work she mostly saw him. With Nim happy at his school, she was working regular shifts, and although Graeme and a young registrar handled the doctors' duties, Malik appeared from time to time, usually inveigling her away to the staffroom so he could sit and spend a few minutes with her.

But this seeing and not touching grew harder with every visit, and her uncertainty about the future threw a shadow on the happiness that being with him here in Madan had so unexpectedly brought her.

Nim was happy, friends coming to play, chattering away in both languages with almost equal fluency. And her? Well, she certainly enjoyed her work in the fairy castle, enjoyed seeing children's faces light up as she came in, and loved the shy greetings from the mothers and aunts and grandmas usually in attendance on the sick children.

Even the fathers, and other male visitors, were accepting of her—perhaps seeing her uniform of loose trousers, tunic and cap as the armour she'd once fancied her uniform at home had been.

Not that it had worked against Malik.

And as if thinking his name had conjured his presence, suddenly he was there, in front of her.

'Come,' he said. 'I have caught up on my sleep, have begged Graeme to spare you to me, and I am taking you up the mountains. I have been a most remiss host, showing you nothing of my country, just setting you to work practically from the time you arrived.'

'And Nim, is he coming?'

'Not today, for this afternoon his class is coming to see the leopard cubs and his excitement—well, he will tell you.'

He paused, then added, 'He will be quite safe, you must believe that.'

And Lauren did, for she knew there were trusted men posted at the school to keep an eye on him, and within the walls of the big estate he would be carefully but unobtrusively watched. Had known too about the class visit to their house but had forgotten, as she did most things, when Malik had appeared.

She smiled at this man who had taken so much worry off her shoulders and brought her to this magical place. Yes, things had been hectic, and marriage seemed no closer, but the rare time they did spend together was—precious?

Certainly, it was drawing them closer, and as far as Lauren was concerned, yes, precious *was* the right word.

Forget the 'if' and live for the moment—go see the mountains.

'I'll just have a wash and be right with you,' she said, and darted off, wishing she'd had the forethought to bring a prettier outfit to the hospital just in case an occasion like this should arise.

But she washed her face and brushed her hair, noticing the curly mop longer now, framing her face more, tickling her neck.

I must ask Keema about getting it cut, she thought as she walked back to Malik, because thinking about mundane things was steadying the dizzy feeling of excitement in her chest.

* * *

She was so lovely, Malik thought, glancing at her when he could while she looked out the window, delighting in all she saw. Goats and camels mostly, until they left the fertile land around the oasis and began to climb the mountains.

'All our land was mountains once,' he told her, 'until wind and rain over thousands of years reduced the stone to sand. Only the strongest rock remained, but it too will one day disappear.'

The road wound upwards, Lauren still intent on the scenery, until he pulled up in the parking area at the top and she could look around, mostly at the vast sky above them and…

'An ocean of desert, the dunes the waves, stretching for ever…' she murmured.

The wonder in her voice touched something in his heart, but rather than bring him joy it caused an ache deep inside him.

How could he not have guessed that whoever it was who'd wanted Tariq dead would not also plot to thwart his plans for marriage?

Because that was what was happening. The whole 'marrying a Madani woman' thing the elders were debating hadn't just arisen out of nowhere. Their rulers had been marrying people from other tribes and nations right down through the generations, yet now when he wanted—really wanted—to marry Lauren, they were bringing in the new law.

He opened the car door and helped her out, putting his arm around her shoulders, leading her to the low wall surrounding the lookout.

'Oh, there's the oasis right beneath us,' she said, delight in her voice. 'And the hospital—the fairy castle, too—and way over there, glinting in the sun, all the big hotels waiting for their tourists.'

He laughed and pulled her closer, his body reacting to

her closeness, wanting her, all of her, but this was hardly the place to be starting something they couldn't finish—hardly the place to be caught kissing in public should someone else arrive to see the view. Madan might be crawling towards modernisation, but public displays of affection?

The Madanis weren't ready for that yet.

'But tourists *should* come,' she said, easing away so she could look at him—following her conversation, not his thoughts. 'Because even the little I've seen of it is beautiful and special. Special interest tourism perhaps, so groups come to learn about the culture, and the people who have lived here since the days of the Silk Road. There's history here, and beauty, things beyond fast-food outlets and fancy hotels.'

Forget someone coming to see the view and local customs. Forget showing public displays of affection. The words she'd just spoken told him she was beginning to understand his homeland—maybe even beginning to love it.

And his joy was so great, how could he not think to hell with protocol and draw her into his arms, this wise woman he so wanted to be his? He kissed her, gently at first, a thank-you-for-those-words kiss, then he kissed her with his heart involved, trying to tell her how he felt—how much he—

Loved?

The word had certainly been there in his thoughts but he pushed it away, substituting wanted her, no matter the obstacles being put in the way.

Could he talk to her about it?

Explain?

But she had given up her old life for him—coming with him to Madan. How could he bother her with the shenanigans going on at the palace?

And was that really his reason for staying silent, for dealing with it on his own? Or was it the centuries of Madani blood in his veins that decreed such things were the business of the man of the family?

He had been educated in the Western world and believed in the equality of men and women, but that inbred Madani pride kept him from burdening her with problems that he, alone, could solve...

For Lauren, the kiss warmed all the places the 'if' had turned cold, and fired the senses Malik so easily aroused, but they were in a public place so they broke apart and walked around the outlook side by side, decorum keeping them a few inches apart.

But sensuality could zap across a few inches and her body ached for him.

He took her home after their brief tryst, and stayed to eat cakes with Nim and his friends from school, a picnic laid out by the kitchen staff on mats in the shade of a large apricot tree.

The children chattered around him, and Nim grew noticeably straighter and taller as his uncle, as he knew him, sat beside him.

And when the feasting finished, while Nim said farewell to his friends, Lauren walked with Malik back to his car.

'There is more than your concern about the state of your nation worrying you,' she said quietly, and he looked at her and smiled.

'I will work it out,' he said. 'I would speak of it if I could, but it is not our way, but I *will* work it out!

He kissed her swiftly on the lips.

'Trust me on that!' he said, and she found herself believing him.

Then he was gone and she could only wait, wondering how long it would be before she would see him again, how long before they could kiss again, make love again—

slowly this time—enjoying the discovery of each other, skin on skin.

She shivered as desire coursed through her. It was probably better if they didn't kiss again—not until everything was sorted and they could be together properly…

For ever?

Right now, for ever didn't matter, though she longed for that with all her heart. But even a part-time relationship with Malik would be better than none at all.

Was this love?

Was this how Lily had felt about Tariq?

Had a kiss made her bones melt?

A touch send fire through her body?

At the hospital, with the measles epidemic waning, Lauren was now on regular shifts, and although previously she'd been called to wherever she was needed most in either of the hospitals, she was now back where she felt she belonged, nursing children.

The little girl with encephalitis was off her drip and recovering slowly, but because she needed to be kept quiet for a few weeks, she was still in the hospital. The lad with the club foot was allowed home, his ankle and lower leg still in a cast so he moved, with surprising speed, on small crutches. The other children she'd met on her first visit had mostly been discharged.

Lauren, who even in the children's hospital was moved around, was on duty in the emergency department— depleted of a number of staff because of the overtime everyone had worked during the measles epidemic.

She wasn't even sure she had someone who spoke English to interpret for her, and, as her own lessons had been interrupted while they'd been so busy, she was worrying about this when a group of people, young and old, came in. She was used to the locals and their manner of dress—the women usually in the loose trousers and tunics, scarves around their heads, while the men wore much the same, only their trousers would be striped and their headgear a cap or intricately wound turban of some kind.

But this group were bright with colour, the women in flaring skirts of purple and orange, pretty blouses on the top, the men in the striped trousers but with bright jackets of red, or blue, or orange, while the barefooted children, pressed shyly against the adults' legs, all wore simple tunics in the striped material of the men's trousers.

As Lauren moved towards them, one of the men stepped forward and said something she didn't understand, but it was clear from his gestures he wanted to see someone else.

Graeme had been here long enough to know the language, but he was having some much-needed time off so Lauren gestured to one of the aides to speak to the group.

The aide spoke to a man who held a young child in his arms, the limpness of the little body suggesting he or she was far from well. Then, with the man in the lead, the group followed the aide to a cubicle, Lauren tagging along behind, aware she'd have to be the one to examine the child.

The child, a girl Lauren discovered when she pushed her way to the front of the group, lay on an examination couch, the man guarding her, the others still clustered around.

'They have to go,' Lauren said to the aide, waving her arms in a shooing motion and wishing she knew more local words, wishing she was a faster learner.

The aide proved her worth, although the protests were voluble enough for Lauren to know they objected to being pushed out.

The aide returned and together they removed the child's tunic. She was so hot to the touch Lauren knew drugs alone wouldn't reduce her temperature, so she mimed washing down the child while she dissolved some dispersible aspirin in water, drew it up into a syringe, and eased it into the child's mouth, sitting her up a little so she could swallow.

'We must cool her,' she said to the father as they worked, and wondered if the aide knew enough English to translate, for she was saying something to the man.

'Now I look at her throat,' Lauren said, opening her own mouth and pointing to the back of it. She lifted a spatula to hold down the tongue and shone a small torch into the mouth.

The tell-tale inflammation of the tonsils and white spots at the back of the throat suggested an infection and for the child to be so ill, a streptococcus infection was a good bet, but Lauren took a swab for testing to be sure.

She checked the girl's ears, but there was no apparent problem there, and all the while her mind worried around one word, penicillin.

Would the man—presumably her father—know if she was allergic to it? The chances were she'd never had it, so no one would know.

But penicillin was the most effective treatment for strep bacteria, which might already be causing inflammation throughout the girl's body, particularly in the joints.

She left the aide sponging the girl down and went in search of the young registrar.

'So what do you think?' she asked him when she'd explained the dilemma.

'Phone Dr Madani,' was his reply, and Lauren couldn't blame the young man. He was only on a rotation through the children's ED, and probably had little hands-on experience with children.

Dr Madani's phone number was readily available, yet Lauren was reluctant to call. He knew her as a capable paediatric nurse—would he expect her to handle it?

And what matter of government business might he be involved in that she'd be interrupting?

Taking up his time when he'd already spent so much time at the hospital.

She phoned Dr Madani.

'Lauren, you are all right? Nimr?'

Wasted minutes with assurances, trying to brush away his concern so she could ask about the child.

'There's no one here to interpret,' she explained to him. 'I know she has a fever and what looks like a strep throat, but I'm wondering about using penicillin. I also need to know how she's feeling—if her joints are aching, that kind of thing.'

'Put the father on the phone,' Malik said, and Lauren sighed with relief, although deep inside she knew this wasn't good enough. She *had* to make more effort to learn the language—and practise more—in order to truly help these people.

But she passed the phone to the father, waited while Malik spoke to him, then the father handed back the phone.

'Were you thinking rheumatic fever?' he asked, and Lauren nodded, then realised she needed to speak and said yes.

'Go with the penicillin. Her joints *are* hurting, but admit her and we'll think about steroids for her joints when we see how she's doing. Keep up the aspirin until her temperature comes down, and, Lauren...'

He paused and she waited.

'They are tribal people, nomads, and it will be hard for them to understand she has to stay in hospital. I have told the father, but the two people only with the child policy isn't going to work.'

Lauren thanked him and pocketed her phone. She drew up penicillin and, explaining as best she could, injected it into the child. She started a drip to keep fluid levels up, and wrote up the instructions on the chart that would go with the child to the ward.

But when it came time to transfer the girl, she went along

with the orderly, wanting to make sure she would be settled in a room so her family could stay with her.

'It's impossible,' Kate, the sister on duty in the ward, grumbled at her. Kate was South African, and was working here as part of a working holiday that would take her around the world, pausing here because she was now engaged to an American oil man. 'The family will give her whatever remedies they think will make her better.'

'If they've been doing it down through many generations, whatever they give her probably won't make her worse,' Lauren said. 'At least they've accepted that whatever they usually use hasn't worked because here she is in hospital.'

Kate continued to mutter under her breath, but Lauren knew she'd see the girl was well looked after. But Malik had been right, there were at least eight people in the room with the patient, and that wasn't counting a tiny baby, hidden in a sling under one of the women's robes.

Her shift ended slightly later than it should have, and, knowing Nim would already be in bed, she went back to the ward to check on the young girl.

To her surprise, the crowd in the room had cleared, although the man she'd taken for the father remained there, sitting cross-legged on the floor, his back against the wall, his dark eyes constantly moving about the room as if some danger might lurk near his child.

'Has he eaten anything?' she asked the nurse who came in to check the drip.

'Not a thing,' she said, 'although we offered him some food.'

'But not food he would like,' a deep voice said, and Malik appeared in the doorway.

He spoke briefly to the man, who replied at far greater length, then apparently started to argue with Malik.

Lauren let it go on for a minute, but as their voices rose,

she pointed to the child and ushered them both towards the door.

All this for a meal?

Finally, the voices stopped and Malik re-entered the room.

'He is particular about what he eats and his wife will have prepared his meal, but he felt he could not leave his child.'

Lauren caught on at once, and shook her head.

'So you have offered to stay with her while he eats?' she guessed. 'In spite of the fact you've hardly slept in more than a week, and are probably in need of feeding yourself!'

He smiled at her and shook his head.

'But you are also here,' he said, 'and that, for me right now, is more than food or sleep.'

Lauren could only smile and shake her head, the beauty of the meaning of the words flooding warmth into her innermost being—into her very soul...

And if the 'if,' whatever it might be, happened or didn't happen, she'd always have those words tucked into her heart to warm lonely nights and bring cheer on hectic days...

CHAPTER NINE

WITH THE MAN GONE, Malik examined the little girl, gently pressing on her knees and ankles, searching for signs of swelling.

He was reaching for the chart when Lauren said quietly, 'I've sent a swab from her throat to the lab and asked for it to be put through as soon as possible, and I've booked her for Radiology tomorrow.'

She grinned at him.

'So it's a good thing you're here so you can explain those things to the father when he comes back and he doesn't think we're kidnapping her when we take her across to the old hospital. I've asked for chest X-rays to check her heart and lungs, and an ECG in case it's already affecting her heart.'

'You don't need me, then,' Malik teased, because he wanted to see her smile again.

'Oh, we definitely need you when it comes to explanations. I've come across men at home who'd prefer a man told them what was happening with their child because there are still men who think another man will know better, but this man? I couldn't tell him the sun would rise in the morning, because even if I spoke the language he wouldn't believe me.'

Malik reached out and touched her shoulder, wishing he could hold her, willing himself not to.

'That man and all the men that came before him *had* to be head of the family. Our people have always been aware of danger. And when there's danger, there must be a leader—one person who tells the others what to do so you don't get panic and mayhem. It is how they have always lived. How *we* have always lived.'

'And because there's been no one ruler since your father died, what you have now is panic and mayhem?' Lauren said.

'Total chaos,' he answered, and thought maybe he could take her in his arms, hold her for just an instant, but before he could move the door opened and the man returned, accompanied by an older woman.

The child's grandmother?

Malik explained about the tests they would do in the morning, about having to take the little girl through the corridor between the hospitals, and, yes, he could go with her.

'Are you off duty?' he asked Lauren, thinking even if she wasn't he'd find someone to replace her. He couldn't just walk away from her now he'd seen her.

'An hour ago,' she told him with a smile, and he touched her hand, just fleetingly, as they walked together to the desk for her to sign out.

'Then we shall go and eat,' he announced. 'We will go to the market—which, yes, I did close, but it has since re-opened—and we will eat as our nomad friend will have eaten tonight. You and Nimr, because my mother fancied food of other countries and her kitchen staff reflect that in what they serve, haven't tasted many of our dishes.'

'You'd be better off grabbing a sandwich—which your mother's staff do very well—and getting some sleep,' she said, concern for him evident in her eyes.

'I will sleep when we have eaten,' he promised. 'I will

even send for another car to take you home, so I am not tempted to do other than sleep should I go first to your place.'

But as they were now in the shadowy dark of the car park he could put his arm around her shoulders and draw her close, feeling her body warm against his, feeling his own respond predictably.

He sighed.

This was not how it should be. They should be married by now, and he'd be taking his excitement home and bedding her—touching her, teasing her, learning what she liked, and what made her cry out—

Al'ama! What was he thinking?

He clicked open the car and opened the door for her, careful now not to touch her lest it inflame already overheated desires.

But to take her now—to lie with her at the house again, not married to him—would bring shame on her and, by implication, on Nimr. To do it once was bad enough and although the memory of that brief encounter was burned into his very bones so he ached whenever they were together, he would not, could not, repeat it.

His staff might be loyal, but gossip was the lifeblood of his people. He would not have her the subject of that, would not have her talked about in the market.

It had happened, yes—that heated, irresistible evening— but no more until they were married, and if that meant avoiding opportunities to be alone with her, then that was what he must do.

So why are you taking her to dinner?

He ignored the question that had whispered in his head, because he knew the answer.

He *needed* to be with her, needed it like he needed air to breathe and water to drink.

And he *was* rationing their contact, trying to see as little as possible of her.

He sighed as he slid behind the wheel, and she reached out and touched his knee.

'Is it so very hard, sorting out the problems you have at the palace?'

He rested his hand on hers, squeezed her fingers and turned towards her, tucking a wayward curl behind her delicate ear.

'Not nearly as hard as sorting out how I can be with you and not have you in my arms. Not holding you, making love to you, sharing talk, and love, and laughter with you.'

She returned the pressure on his fingers and said, 'You could always walk away, come back to Australia, live with us there as a normal family.'

He was wondering whether that could be a realistic option, when she leaned across and kissed him softly on the cheek.

'But I know you wouldn't,' she said softly. 'Back when we first met, you told me of the things you desperately wanted to achieve for your country. It was the reason you gave to need Nim back here in Madan. I heard the passion in your voice as you spoke of your plans, and it stirred something inside me.'

She touched her fingers to his cheek, his lips.

'To leave, to walk away from those dreams and aspirations, you wouldn't be that man who spoke with such passion of his people and their needs. You wouldn't be the man I've come to know so well and, I think, to love. So we stay, and pretend, and surely, one day, things will work out and we can be properly together.'

'A normal family,' he repeated, his voice gruff as a rarely felt emotion had tightened his throat as she'd told him of her love…

* * *

The markets were alive with lights, colour and music. Booths pushed against each other, selling everything from hair shampoo to enormous silver urns and vases, with clothing, car tyres, toys and radios in between.

'It's mad,' Lauren murmured, staying close to Malik as she feared she'd never find him in the crush should they be separated.

'Through this way,' he said, and steered her down a side alley to where the businesses were more substantial, tucked into the ground floor of buildings so they had doors that could be shut at night, if night actually closed the markets down.

Another alley then into a building and through a dark corridor that opened into a magnificent courtyard.

'I cannot believe that this is hidden away in here, in the midst of the madness that is the markets.'

'Most of the houses are like this, nothing but a building on the outside, but inside—'

He waved his hand to indicate the scene in front of them, the floor and walls bright with glazed tiles set in patterns as intricate as the carpets they walked on at the house, the potted palms and other small trees tucked here and there, the small fountain against one wall, and bright orange, and purple, and green cushions, large enough to lounge on, scattered here and there.

'There are tables if you'd rather,' Malik said, but seeing the small groups of people sitting on the cushions, each area made a little private by the potted plants, she opted for a cushion and they sat, Malik speaking to the woman who had greeted them.

'You will let me choose?' he said to Lauren, who smiled and nodded, still captivated by the beauty of the courtyard inside what had looked like a very drab exterior.

The woman returned to spread a mat, which looked far

too beautifully woven to serve as a tablecloth, between them, then set down a silver jug, the outside frosted with beads of condensation, promising something cold inside.

She poured drinks, pale pink in colour and tangy with lemon, though the other ingredients Lauren could only guess at.

They raised their glasses in a toast, though to what she didn't want to think. It was enough to be with Malik, to sit a while, and eat and drink, and not worry about what might lie ahead.

Whatever happened, she knew that Nim was safe, and just knowing that had freed so much of the tension inside her that the future held no terrors.

Small nibbly things appeared—roasted nuts, dates, of course, but filled with a kind of soft cheese, olives, warmed in oil and lemon, flavoured with herbs that, again, she didn't know, and tiny, spicy meatballs, with delicious, cool yoghurt to dip them in.

'I've had to try everything and won't be able to eat anything else,' she told him, and he smiled.

'I think you will, when it arrives.'

Someone cleared away the dishes on the mat before the first woman returned with a strange-shaped earthenware dish and a bowl of couscous—pearl couscous Lauren remembered it was called—the bigger version. Pomegranate seeds and thin slices of preserved lemon skin decorated the top of the couscous, but as the woman lifted the lid of the other dish, the aroma of a very special meal had Lauren forgetting anything else.

There must be spices in it she didn't know, but she recognised saffron, and something sweeter.

'Try a little,' Malik suggested, putting a spoonful of couscous on her plate as the woman put a small amount of the stew—the only name Lauren had for it—with it.

She tried it, breathing in the spice-filled aroma. The

meat was tender and delicious—lamb?—but with dried apricots, softened by long cooking, and tiny sultanas, carrot chunks, and another vegetable that Lauren couldn't name.

'It's delicious,' she said, passing her plate back to the woman's waiting hand, watching as she piled it high, holding up her hand so it didn't get even higher.

Malik was served, although Lauren imagined he would normally be served first, and together they ate, silent at first as they revelled in the exotic food.

But as appetite was satisfied they slowed, and talked, of food and the hospital and Malik's plans to get better education out to the far reaches of Madan, to build a university to train teachers and nurses and doctors.

'Shall we walk a little?' Malik suggested, when they'd finished their meal with a tiny cup of coffee.

He led her further into the market until they came out into the open, close by the darkness of the oasis, moonlight reflecting the palm grove in the still waters.

And hand in hand they wandered into the welcoming shadows beneath the thick-topped palms, the sweet smell of ripening dates filling the air with an intoxicating perfume.

And where a tiny trail led closer to the water, Malik took her in his arms and held her.

At first content to be close, Lauren's body remembering his, heating at the memory, until, inevitably, they were kissing, desperate kisses that told of yearning and frustration.

They held each other tightly, bound by their attraction.

Love?

But though she might not know details—would he ever share his concerns with her? See her as a full partner in their relationship?—she knew there were forces around them who could put an end to Malik's plans for his country, his hopes and dreams for Madan.

'I will sort it soon,' he promised when they eased apart, then kissed again because how could they not?

They walked back to the car, not through the markets but through the date palms, pausing now and then to kiss—to be together. But when they reached the car, Lauren's mind turned back to work.

'We should give the girl and all her family the measles vaccine. We're still getting a few cases,' she said, and Malik laughed.

'What's so funny?' she demanded.

'My mind is still on you—on kisses—and you? You're thinking work!'

'I was thinking there could still be some infection around and those people will be vulnerable, the young girl particularly so. Would it hurt to give her the vaccination while she's already fighting off the staph infection? Her body will see the vaccine as a further invasion and might fight it.'

Malik forgot about discretion and gave her a hug.

'Yes, we'll vaccinate the family, and the girl too, but as you say, not yet. And I'll find out from the leader where other tribes might be. They all come into the city from time to time, so they should all be protected, preferably before they arrive. How to do it is something I've been puzzling over, but with the need right now, I'll figure something out.'

He spoke lightly, but the idea excited him, for it had thrown up possibilities he hadn't considered.

He was getting nothing but frustration from the council, and the trade route the nomads still travelled was close to the lodge he had built when they had been setting the first of the young leopards free in their natural habitat.

He wouldn't leave until they had the results of the tests on the young girl and had stabilised her, but after that...

'I'll arrange vaccinations for the family and track down where some of the other nomadic tribes might be. They are very regular in their travel so we should be able to go out to the camps and vaccinate them before they get too close to town.'

He walked beside her to the car, his mind racing and excitement burning in his body. He would leave his two most trusted men with Nimr, let the housekeepers who lived at his lodge know that they were coming so they could open up the lodge and get in food.

Should he tell Lauren of his plans?

He shook his head at the thought. He'd already brought her here with a promise of marriage that, up until now, he'd been unable to keep, and in the current warring climate in the palace, who knew what might arise to thwart that plan.

So he hugged his excitement to himself, although as he kissed her goodnight in the shadows of the colonnade, he hoped his kiss told her of his feelings, if not his plans…

CHAPTER TEN

WITH YET ANOTHER meeting of the council of elders set down for ten days' time, Malik made his plans. He had loyal men who would lobby council members while he was away, and already he had close to a majority to vote against the new motion.

Graeme was delighted with the idea of having the nomadic people vaccinated, suggesting they might do other inoculations at the same time and organising all the equipment and drugs they would need.

'You'll take Lauren?' Graeme asked, and Malik studied his old mentor for a moment, wondering how much he knew or guessed about the situation—the delayed marriage, and his, Malik's, growing passion for the woman he'd brought so far.

Malik nodded.

'She did well organising everyone at the house,' he said, and wondered if it had sounded like an excuse and whether he should have said nothing.

But Graeme just smiled.

'That's good, she needs a break,' he said. 'She's bonded well with the family of the little girl—she seems to understand the people she'll be dealing with.'

Was that another dilemma? Something that might thwart his plan?

Malik shook off any doubts. Once the rheumatic fever diagnosis had been proved by tests, Lauren had been spending most of her on-duty hours with the child and her family.

But no one worked twenty-four hours a day, so other nurses were familiar with the case, and as the penicillin had reduced the swelling and pain in the girl's throat and she was eating well, there was little nursing to do.

Nevertheless, it was Lauren's first objection when he came to her with his idea of taking her out to the nomad camp on the old Silk Road to vaccinate the people there before they came into town.

'We'll be away a few days,' he told her, 'and I have already explained to the family of the sick girl that another nurse will be with her. And you can be sure Nimr will be well cared for. He tells me he would like his friend Najeeb to stay, so perhaps this would be a good time to have him over so he doesn't miss you so much.'

Lauren smiled at him.

'You don't leave much for me to do, then. Nim hasn't stopped talking about having Najeeb to stay, and you're right, this would be an ideal time.'

She guessed there was more to this than a simple trip out into the desert, that Malik had everything so organised before she'd even known about it. But whatever lay ahead, with Nim happy with the arrangements, it was a trip she'd love to make.

The two boys would have both Aneesha and Keema to look after them, and Lauren knew there'd be trusted men around them all the time.

'So,' she finally said, when she'd settled all of this in her head and faced Malik again, 'exactly what are you planning?'

The smile he gave her and the reaction of her body to that smile told her all she needed to know.

She closed her eyes to take it in, and tamped down the excitement that frustration had been building in her body.

'We stay in the camp?' she asked, and received an even more explicit smile in reply.

'You will see,' he said. 'It will be a surprise for you.'

And it was all she could do to *not* leap into his arms and hug him, hold him, kiss him…

Most unseemly behaviour in a hospital corridor.

She saw no more of Malik that day, eating dinner with Nim, who was so excited about having his friend to stay over he could barely eat his food.

But the excitement proved enough to send him straight to sleep, and Lauren was free to sit in her bedroom and consider what she should pack for a few working days with, as far as she could make out, a little extracurricular excitement thrown in.

Gloom set in. Okay, so she had plenty of respectable loose trousers and tunics like the ones she now wore all the time, but they were far from sexy.

For the past four years, her life had revolved around Nim and keeping him safe, so sexy underwear had been the furthest thing from her mind. But hers were so darned functional they made her want to weep.

So she did, just a little, and was drying her eyes when Keema entered to tell her Malik would like to see her.

He was waiting, very properly, in the small salon where she and Nim usually watched television.

'I thought I might see him to say goodbye, but it seems he's asleep already,' he said as she came into the room.

Then as she came closer he took her hands and drew her to him, looking down into her face.

'You have been crying? You are worried about leaving Nim? *Al'ama*, I am so stupid. I think only of myself and my own desires to be alone with you for a little time. It is too hard for you?'

He sounded so concerned Lauren put her hand to his cheek and kissed him swiftly on the lips.

'No, I'm fine, and Nim is so happy about the arrangement, he will not realise I'm gone.'

They talked a while and then he left, finalising the time he would send a car for her, explaining they would travel in his helicopter to the camp.

Another quick kiss and he was gone.

She shut away the doubts, packed her case, then showered and washed her hair, uncertain about what facilities a desert camp might have.

The nomad camp, when they arrived, made Lauren shake her head in disbelief. The tents themselves, large rounded affairs, were black, made from some kind of tanned animal skin, but all around was a swirl of colour.

Bright carpets were spread on the sand, women and children in brilliantly coloured outfits moved around outside the tents, while more carpets and mats hung from the anchoring ropes.

Camels wandered nearby, hobbles between their front feet preventing them from straying, and further out, a makeshift fence and a number of small boys kept goats and horses corralled.

A tall man, his head covered in a black turban with a long tail, appeared from the larger of the tents, and came towards the helicopter.

'You are welcome in my camp, Abdul-Malik,' he said, with a slight bow of his head.

'I am honoured to be here,' Malik replied, and while Lauren was trying to work out why the pair was speaking English, Malik spoke again.

'You will have heard many people in the city have been ill with the measles epidemic, a number of them seriously ill. I have brought a nurse to help me and we will vaccinate your people so they need not fear that illness or many others.'

'I have heard that too, and that you were coming,' the man said. 'You and the nurse from Australia, I believe.'

He turned to bow his head at Lauren, who held out her hand.

'I am Lauren,' she said, smiling at the man. 'And do you hear these things through some age-old tradition of listening to the wind, or do you have mobile phones these days?'

He laughed and dug into the pocket of his gown, to produce one of the latest models of phone.

'Easier than listening to the wind, although we still listen to it as well, for it tells us other things.'

Intrigued, Lauren couldn't help herself.

'Like sandstorms?' she said, and the man nodded once more.

'Those, and other travellers in our vicinity—the wind also tells us that.'

It was Lauren's turn to nod. She had read enough to know that in times when wars had been fought over territorial rights or bridal dowries, knowing an enemy was close would be important.

Malik was explaining how they planned to carry out the vaccinations, and the man had sent several young men to the helicopter to collect the ice boxes and medical equipment.

The man strode away to organise his people.

'His English is so—English, I suppose. Was he educated there?'

Malik smiled.

'He was at school with me in England. He lives this life by choice, but also so he can indulge in his love of archaeology. He doesn't look for treasure but for everyday things people in the past made use of in their daily lives. One day he hopes to set up a museum that will track the lives of all who used the Silk Road over the centuries.'

Lauren shook her head in amazement.

'That would surely take more than one man's lifetime!'

Malik smiled at her.

'Ah, but you do not know this man,' he said.

He was certainly a good organiser, Lauren realised when he returned to show them to a small shelter that had been erected, with a folding table and chairs and two young women standing by, presumably to fetch and carry anything she or Malik might need, and to keep records of the patients.

And queues were already forming outside the shelter, women with small children at the front, then the men and boys, and at the end older people, possibly reluctant to be there.

'So, I have explained and you may start,' the leader said to them when he appeared from nowhere in front of them.

Lauren unpacked the equipment box, setting alcohol wipes in front of each of them, the ice boxes of vaccines between them, and two sharps containers behind those. They had a jar of hand sanitiser each and a box of gloves, and, tucked down in a box she left between the two chairs, jars containing jelly beans to give the children.

'At least we've had some practice at mass vaccination,' she said to Malik as they began—the measles, mumps and rubella vaccine the first they gave to everyone.

The young girls brought each patient forward and instructed them to roll up his or her sleeve, then, with the injection done, ushered the patient out through the open back of the shelter before writing in their notebooks.

In the early afternoon the queues disappeared. There one minute and gone the next.

'Lunch,' the headman announced. 'Come!'

Once out of the shelter, Lauren realised how hot the day had become.

'You will rest when you have eaten,' the man commanded, and Lauren knew it was a good idea.

'For an hour,' Malik said. 'No longer, for we wish to finish all the MMR vaccinations today. Tomorrow we will start on triple antigens for the babies and children, and for those to be effective we will need to return again and again.'

'And tetanus?' Lauren asked, ashamed she'd been so caught up in her longings for sexy lingerie she hadn't thought to ask Malik the details of the inoculations they'd be doing.

He smiled at her.

'I did that many years ago—when I was still a student. A group of us, friends of mine, used it as a holiday placement. We had a four-wheel drive bus and set out along the nomadic tribes' favoured routes. We had no hope of covering all the camps, but it's a tradition that's continued, and at each camp we would train a couple of people to give the injections and leave a small supply. Now they can replenish that supply when they are camped close to a town or city.'

Lauren could only shake her head, imagining the young medical students on their trek across the wild, uninhabited plains.

They rested in the main tent, on rugs piled on each other, made more comfortable by fat cushions. The two young women reclined by Lauren, who realised with an inward smile that Malik was ensconced on his throne of mats on the far side of the tent.

He was speaking with the headman and Lauren sensed the talk, in their own language, was a serious one.

The rest hour ended with cool drinks and sweet pastries, then it was back to work until the sun began to set, its red orb turning the desert into a field of flame.

'There is a solar-powered freezer where the cool boxes

can be stored,' the headman told them. 'And I have asked my driver to take you to the lodge. He will collect you in the morning.'

He held up his hand to forestall Malik's protest.

'I know you know the way, but these days you are a city man—let me keep you safe.'

He bowed quite deeply as he spoke and Lauren guessed Malik had spoken to him of his problems with the palace.

If so, it was evident he had this man's support—but would that count in palace circles? Was this man even a citizen of Madan, or were nomadic tribes stateless, governed by the rule of the tribe?

'We will sit in the back,' Malik said, as he led Lauren to the big four-wheel drive vehicle. 'To do otherwise would embarrass our driver.'

He opened the door and took Lauren's hand to help her up, felt the tremor in her fingers as he touched her, and his own nerves respond immediately.

But what he'd planned would not be hurried. They were greeted at the lodge by the couple who lived there, looking after the place and also tracking the released leopards through small transmitters placed under the animals' skin. In the main room, a large map took up most of the wall, and Malik led Lauren to it, explaining its purpose and showing her the paths the released animals followed.

And as he watched her follow one track with a finger, her face showing her fascination in this, his pet project, he knew he loved her more deeply than he'd known he could love, and refused to consider there could be any other option than marrying her.

Marla led her to the guest bedroom, and Malik smiled to himself as he imagined her reaction to the palatial space, with the huge, netting-shrouded bed and gleaming bathroom beside it.

'You have all this out here in the desert?'

He heard the disbelief in her voice and walked over to the doorway, Marla ducking out as he stood there.

'My mother loved this place and, as you already know, she wasn't one to stint on luxuries. With bores sunk deep into the desert for water and solar panels for power, this was my mother's idea of camping.'

'Are all the rooms like this?' Lauren asked, then he saw colour rise to her cheeks, and he guessed she was wondering where he would sleep.

'Not quite as luxurious and the beds are definitely not as comfortable,' he said, stepping towards her and putting an arm around her shoulders to draw her close. 'So perhaps we'll have to share.'

She shivered and he wondered just how inexperienced she probably was. Before Lily's death there'd probably been boyfriends but the last four years, when she might have been learning more of the ways of men and women, had been stolen from her by her need to keep Nimr safe.

He kissed her cheek, her nose, her forehead and finally her lips, which parted like a parched man's seeking water. And through their tunics he felt the hard nubs of her breasts, and heard the tiny sigh she gave when his tongue touched hers.

And for a moment his determination to make love to her slowly and sensually wavered and he pictured himself lifting her through the screens around the bed and—

'I will leave you here to have a bath and rest before dinner,' he said, easing her away from his body and dropping a parting kiss on her lips. 'There is a deck out front, we can sit there to eat, so come through when you are ready.'

By the time Lauren joined him on the deck, wearing the blue trousers and tunic that was Nim's favourite, a nearly full moon was rising in the sky, turning the sands silver with its light.

Malik was seated at a low table, and he stood, hand out-held, to help her to a chair, so they could sit together and look out at the magic of the desert at night, where flashes of shadow suggested small animals might be hunting in the cool air of the evening.

The table was laden with silver platters, all with domed silver covers over them.

'It's like a game—lifting the covers to see what's un-derneath,' Lauren said, and Malik smiled at her, his eyes telling her things she longed to hear from his lips.

Or maybe she was just carried away, and it was nothing more than moonlight glinting in his eyes...

Until he touched her, just lightly on the shoulder, and said the words.

'I love you!'

But now the words she'd longed to hear sent her into a panic. What to do? What to say?

And did he mean it?

Was that question the reason why the words had thrown her so much? Shouldn't she have been thrilled, excited, throwing herself into his arms and telling him she loved him too?

She'd accepted some time ago that what she felt for him was love, but she'd never considered his care of her, his consideration, even the attraction between them might be signs of his love for her...

Thoughts and words chased through her head and she shook it to clear it, but that didn't help.

Maybe he had guessed at her confusion that he said, 'Let's eat,' and lifted one of the covers to show a mound of golden rice, speckled with currants and toasted almonds. He spooned some on a plate and then uncovered a meat dish—tantalisingly spicy—and added a spoonful of that.

'You can help yourself to anything you'd like with it,'

he said, as if the 'I love you' had never been said. 'You will find preserves and pickles under the smaller covers.'

But Lauren was shaking too much to lift a single cover, shaking so much she used two hands to reach for the plate he'd served for her.

'Relax,' he said. 'We will be all right—that I promise you.'

And even though that little 'if' still hovered in the back of her mind, the words did help her relax, and she thanked him—for the words, the food, and for his love.

She set the plate on the table in front of her, then leaned across to kiss him on the lips.

'I love you too,' she said. 'And, yes, we'll work it out.'

Her own lie, really, that last part, for doubt about the outcome of their relationship was alive and well deep inside her, but for now she'd eat and love, and love and smile, and the love would leave her with happy memories, if nothing else...

Well, probably a broken heart, but she wouldn't think about that now, especially as he'd served himself some food but wasn't eating. Instead he was running his finger up her arm, beneath the sleeve of her tunic, and she knew, had her arm been bare as it would have been at home, the feeling could not possibly have been as erotic as this delicate touch beneath her clothing.

CHAPTER ELEVEN

MOONLIGHT FILLED THE room with its silvery magic, making Lauren's skin lustrous as he slipped off her tunic and trousers, the silk material making soft noises as it slid across her skin.

And as he'd promised, Malik took his time, wanting to see her, all of her—the gleaming skin, her pert breasts, a tiny waist and flaring hips.

He touched her, just to feel that skin—feel the warmth of it as the desire he could read in her eyes heated her body.

'My turn to strip you,' she said, but her voice trembled just a little and he knew she was uncertain. So he took her hands and guided them, removing his long tunic and the cloth he wrapped around his hips, so she couldn't help but see how ready for her he was.

But he'd promised to go slowly—to tease and tantalise—and he began with kisses that started on her lips but soon slipped lower to her neck and then her breasts—one and then the other, feeling her tremble now, though the hands that held his head to her were fiercely strong.

He lifted her to the bed and set her down, trailing his fingers now as well as his kisses up and down her body, her legs, her thighs, her belly button, lips kissing still, fingers teasing, touching, prying—opening her to further exploration as she twisted on the bed and uttered little cries that fired his own need even more.

But only when she cried out for him to stop, to not stop, to stop the torment, did he enter her, taking her slowly and carefully, feeling her moist warmth tighten around him, her body in rhythm now with his, until they finally crested the wave of desire together, gasping, crying out, clinging to each other like the survivors of a shipwreck.

He held her, wanting to stay like this for ever, their bodies bonded, their need satisfied for now.

Turning her so she lay by his side, she nestled closer, murmuring his name, looking into his face with a kind of wonder. Then her dark-lashed eyelids drooped and closed and she slept, while he watched over her, and wondered what lay ahead for both of them.

By morning they were sated with love, sleepily holding, touching, stroking each other, reluctant to leave the cocoon of the canopied bed, although work was waiting for them.

As was breakfast when, showered and fresh and slightly shy, Lauren made her way out onto the deck. There were baskets of fresh fruit, platters of cut melons, dishes of yoghurt spiced with nutmeg and sweetened with honey, and silver plates with their domed covers hiding spicy meat dishes and couscous or rice.

She knew her way around the Madan breakfast feast by now, and stuck with the yoghurt and fruit, Malik joining her as she selected a ripe, red strawberry.

He plucked it from her fingers.

'Open wide!'

And popped it in her mouth, so she tasted his skin with the sweet burst from the fruit.

She looked up into his eyes and saw him smile—knew she was smiling too.

* * *

For three idyllic days they worked together at the camp, exploring in the late afternoons, hoping to catch sight of a leopard, happy just to be together, with the curtained bed waiting for them in the lodge.

But that third night Malik was distracted, taking phone calls late into the night, collapsing into bed beside her, holding her tightly to him before turning on his side to sleep, lovemaking lost in his distraction.

She turned towards his unyielding body in the bed they'd shared with such joy and slid her arms around his waist, resting her head against his shoulder.

'Why can't you talk about what's worrying you?' she whispered to him. 'I probably can't help but sometimes talking about a problem will make things clearer. Talk to me—try it?'

Felt his shoulder move as he took in a breath and heard the sigh as it came out.

'Through all our generations there has been a divide—'

He stopped as if he had no idea how to continue.

'Between men and women?' Lauren guessed. 'Between what was men's business and what was women's business?'

She felt his nod and held him close, hoping she could find the right words.

'But the old ways are already changing. You have spoken so passionately about bringing Madan into the twenty-first century.'

'Over time,' he said gruffly, but she could feel his body relaxing.

'So talk to me. I'm already there—I'm a twenty-first-century woman. To me, you sharing your problems would be a gift—a sign of trust. And without trust, how can there be love?'

He turned and took her in his arms.

'It's such a mess that I cannot get it straight in my own

head, let alone explain to you or anyone else. I've told you the elders can make laws and right now they are discussing a law that would sabotage our marriage, which has already been delayed far too long. I know who is behind it—my uncle, spurred on by his wife.'

'And you *know* this?'

'I do, but what I cannot work out is why. If I knew that, I could probably sort it out, but it doesn't make sense because I cannot connect it to Tariq's death. Yet I know from information my informants have given me that the two *must* be connected.'

Lauren wrapped her arms around him and warmed him with her body, her own head trying to make sense of things.

'Are you sure Tariq was the target?'

Malik pulled away from her as if to search her eyes for answers, although the moonlight would reveal little.

'The police—your police—were certain the accident wasn't set up to kill your parents. They looked into that quite deeply.'

It was Lauren's turn to sigh.

'I know all about that part of it—he was the only heir and chief target—I fielded many hours of questions myself. But if it wasn't Tariq or my parents, that only leaves Lily,' she said. 'Although why anyone would want to kill her, I cannot imagine.'

'Lily!'

He breathed the name, but his arms tightened around Lauren, clasping her to him so he could drop a quick kiss on her lips.

Then he was gone, out of bed and out the door, back on his cell phone, his voice urgent, questioning—demanding?

They returned to the city in the morning, Nim and Najeeb welcoming her with cries of delight, both wanting stories

about the nomadic tribe and their camp—and life returned
to normal, although a new normal now.

Aware that Malik had been neglecting things while
they'd been away, she accepted that she wouldn't see much
of him, and their time was reduced to brief glimpses in
hospital corridors, hurried consultations over a sick child.

But even in these almost stolen moments she knew the
bond of love was there between them, and now she understood a little more of the ways of this new country—understood the traditional places held by men and women in it.
Now he'd spoken to her once about the problem, perhaps he
would again, but if not, she wouldn't pester him—wouldn't
force cultural change on him too suddenly. Loving him as
she did, she was content to wait until the business that was
troubling him had been resolved.

He came early one evening to see Nim before he went
to bed, and to walk with her among the roses.

But his face was drawn with worry, his eyes deeply troubled, and though his hand touched hers as they walked, he
didn't take it, didn't hold her and kiss her in the shadows
of the colonnade.

Instead, he pulled a small pocket knife from somewhere
and cut some roses as they walked—white and yellow, pink
and red, a huge bouquet of colour and perfume by the time
they were back at the front steps.

And there he handed them to her, his handkerchief
wrapped around the stems to protect her hands from thorns.

'I caught the scent of roses in your hair that first day we
met,' he said, so serious Lauren felt a quiver of fear in her
heart. 'Now, for ever, you'll be tied to me through roses—
roses and love.'

He took her free hand, lifted it and kissed her fingers,
then departed, the quiver in her heart now a shard of ice,
for his words had sounded like goodbye…

* * *

Malik walked away, aware he should have spoken—trusted her to understand. But how could he tell her that the information was pointing more and more to a member of his family—his uncle's wife—being behind the deaths of her family? *And* the abduction of the child she loved?

How could she, knowing this, hold him in her arms again, make love with him again?

Although not telling her was surely worse.

He shook his head. As yet it was merely suspicion and there was still the vote to be faced, one way or another.

He argued, fought, cajoled the council, but the force behind the clutch of elders wanting the new law was backed now by three of his uncles.

As family they would normally stand behind him, whatever his decision. But this time they couldn't be swayed, so the arguments went back and forth, and the need to shore up *his* supporters was constant, for many of them would prefer to take the easy way out of any decision.

Added to all that was his concern over information still coming in—information that tied, if not his uncle, at least his uncle's wife to the death of Tariq.

Surely not his uncle?

No, that was impossible—wasn't it?

They were family.

He had to try to work it out, to force himself to think beyond the imminent decision to what his uncle could have gained by removing Tariq from the family equation. Nimr would still have been the heir, although maybe they'd hoped he, too, would have been in the vehicle. A two-week-old infant—of course he'd have been with his mother.

Except that Lily had hardly been the maternal type and leaving Nimr with Lauren had meant she could enjoy herself more.

But after Nimr, he, Malik, would have succeeded to the throne—he *was* his father's second son. Would he, too, have been targeted if that had happened?

He pounded his head with an open hand, trying to make his brain chase down through tangled pathways of deceit.

As things stood now, if the proposed change was made to the law, he couldn't marry Lauren *and* rule as regent for Nimr. The suggested law was that the ruler must have a Madani wife, but because it would not be retrospective, Nimr was still the heir.

And in danger?

Malik sighed—there was so much he didn't know, couldn't even guess at.

But what *was* certain was that a regent acted as the ruler, and marriage to Lauren would mean someone else would be appointed regent for Nimr, probably one of the uncles, all of whom were unheeding of the needs of the country.

And one of whom might have been implicated in Tariq's death...

If nothing else, what he was going through now had shown him how archaic their so-called government was—the country run by a group who took care of their own interests first, and could be swayed by favours, gifts and possibly even bribes.

There were only two days now to the vote and Malik wondered how long it would take, should he defeat the motion, to bring democracy to his people so everyone could have a say in how Madan was governed, instead of leaving all important decisions to the ruling tribe.

Lauren was aware that gossip was now rampant in the house, but her language lessons were proceeding slowly.

In the end, she had to ask, seeing Nim off to school then going in search of Keema, wondering how to broach the subject.

But it seemed Keema had already guessed at Lauren's new closeness with Malik, for her voice, as she answered, was heavy with regret.

'There is a new law,' she said. 'The ruler or the regent must marry a Madani woman.'

The words hit Lauren with the force of a lightning bolt, sending her head into a whirl and her heart into palpitations.

Stupid, of course, when she hadn't wanted to marry him in the first place. She'd agreed because of Nim…

But acknowledging stupidity didn't take away the pain.

For herself, for Malik, and for the country he'd hoped to help.

No, that was stupid—he could still rule for Nim, get things organised as he'd intended. Couples broke up all the time, and they'd been together so briefly they probably hadn't reached couple status.

She thanked Keema for her trust in passing on the information, and resolutely set her mind to getting somewhere close to normal. She was on a late shift. She'd go to work and come home, check on Nim, play with him in the morning, then go to work and come home again, and again, and again.

She could handle a simple existence, like the one she'd set herself when she'd stopped running and been determined to lead a normal life for Nim's sake.

But for all she'd been determined to stay strong, after two days all she really wanted was to see Malik—to tell him that it didn't matter.

Should she hold out a hand, stop him, take him somewhere quiet and explain this to him?

But the opportunity failed to arise, and even Nim was asking where he was…

Then one night he was there—early morning, really—pale and shaking by her bed, a sound as slight as a sigh waking her, so she stood up and took him in her arms, dragged him down and loved him all she could, with kisses and touches, and whispers of passion, taking his body and giving hers in return.

He slept then, in her arms, a deep and dreamless sleep, she hoped, but was gone when she awoke, alone and naked in her bed.

Was *this* goodbye?

Was this how her recent dreams of love and marriage would end?

No, she was wrong! She may not have known the man long, but she knew him well. He would not just walk away from her without a word.

He would do what had to be done about the deaths of their families, and he'd sort out the mayhem going on with the elders, because his country depended on him to take it forward. These were his most pressing concerns—and his duty.

And with duty done, he'd come for her.

All she had to do was wait.

He came again, late one afternoon, as she was wandering through the roses. He took her hand and walked with her in silence, until it was time to go inside and have dinner with Nim, who wasn't hesitant in complaining about what he thought had been such a long absence—although it had been all of four days.

'I have been busy,' Malik said, though the lines of strain on his face had already told Lauren that much. 'You know I would have come if I could.'

He included Lauren as he spoke, and she read the agony of uncertainty in his eyes.

He read Nim's bedtime story and they both kissed him goodnight, and as they left the room he took Lauren's hand in his.

'Can we talk a while?' he asked quietly.

And although inside she was such a mess she didn't want to hear his words, she had to know what was going on—and had to hear from him that the dream was over.

'Let's sit outside,' she said, and they walked along the colonnade to where soft cushioned cane chairs were set around small tables.

'Would you like coffee?' she asked, a polite hostess in what really wasn't her home.

He shook his head.

'I'm coffeed out,' he muttered. 'May never touch the stuff again.'

But before he sat he turned towards her, took both her hands and leaned in to kiss her.

Just gently, on the lips—a single kiss—but he kept her hands and somehow they were both sitting on the small lounge chair, hands clinging to each other.

'Have you heard about the law—the vote?' he said, and before she could reply added, 'How could you not—it would have been all over the house, if not the hospital. I know they've talked of nothing in the marketplace for days.'

He sounded so tired she slipped one hand out of his grasp to put it around his shoulders and pull him close.

And waited.

CHAPTER TWELVE

IF ONLY HE could find the words, Malik thought.

If only the decision he'd finally come to didn't hurt so much!

But he had to tell her, explain, find out what would make her happy.

He groaned then straightened his spine, put *his* arm around *her* shoulders, and held her to him.

'The new law makes it impossible for me to marry you and act as regent for Nimr,' he began. 'And the leader of the group that voted for it was one of my uncles. He—all my uncles—are easily bent to stronger wills, which my eldest uncle's wife certainly has.'

He paused, seeking words that weren't full of rage. None of this was Lauren's doing, although he believed now it had revolved around her sister.

'It was you who made me think more clearly about Tariq's death—think it through without emotion. And the question you asked—was I sure he was meant to be the victim?—made me realise that none of us had known he was in Australia. As far as we were all concerned, he was in the US.'

'But the local police ruled out my parents as the target,' Lauren reminded him.

He took a deep breath—there had to be truth for there to be trust.

'And Lily? Did anyone consider her?'

He put his palms against her cheeks, framing her face so he could see her eyes as he explained.

'When I considered Lily, it all became clear. My uncle's wife is from another powerful family, and she and Tariq had been promised to each other as young children.'

Grey eyes widened as she took this in.

'Then Lily came along,' she whispered, and he held her close and smoothed his hands across her hair.

'My information is that she sent three members of her family—distant relatives but trusted—to America and from there they travelled to Australia. Two of them—the couple who took Nim—are still in jail in Australia, and the third could be anywhere for he never returned to Madan.'

Lauren pulled away from him, needing to see his face.

'You *know* all this or is it just supposition?'

'I know most of it,' he said, his voice deep with the sadness this knowledge had brought him. 'She had no idea Tariq would be there—she was simply intent on getting rid of the woman who'd taken the man she thought of as hers.'

'And your uncle married her?'

Now he frowned and shook his head.

'There was dishonour in the family, you see. Although the arrangement wasn't set in stone, to renege would have brought on bad blood between the families. My uncle sorted that by marrying her himself so the families were united, just in a different way.'

'But she wants more?'

He sighed.

'Marriage to Tariq would have made her the wife of the ruler. Without the law, you, the sister of the woman she so hated, would take that role—though as wife of the regent.

I think she could not bear that, especially as the realisation that she'd killed Tariq as well as Lily must have haunted her for the last four years.'

'Poor woman!' Lauren said. 'To be in so much pain she was driven to murder.'

'Poor woman indeed,' Malik snorted. 'I doubt she's felt a single moment of remorse. It is power she wants—power that motivates her.'

'And still wants, if she has persuaded your uncle and his supporters the new law is a good thing for the country. Would it be your uncle who takes control if you were not available?'

Malik nodded.

'Who *will* take control—for I will not be available!'

He spoke so determinedly Lauren shivered.

'Of course you will,' she said, hoping she had kept the pain and anguish she was feeling out of her voice.

Malik held her for a moment, held her close, before telling her the decision that had caused him so many sleepless nights but which was, he felt, the only way to go. 'I have decided we will leave.'

She stiffened against him, opened her mouth to protest, but he closed it with a quick kiss.

'Well, *I* will leave and hope you and Nimr will come with me. We will go back to Australia, or to another country if you wish—go together, marry and become a family—maybe have more children, who knows. I will work and you too if you wish, and we will make a new life for ourselves and forget this place.'

He heard a long sigh, then Lauren turned so she could take his face in the palms of *her* hands and look deep into his eyes.

'You are such a bad liar,' she said, almost smiling at the

same time. 'You know you could never forget this place—this is your home, your country.'

'Maybe deep down in my heart I could not,' he admitted, 'but with you and Nimr we can build a new life and I can grow to love a new country.'

'Nonsense!' Lauren said. 'You'd be useful in another country, doctors always are, but you are *needed* here, by the country, and by the people that you love. You are needed here to help them come to terms with a new future—to help the country grow and develop into a modern society. And you know, in every fibre of your being, that if you go, that will not happen.'

Unable to deny her words, he could only look at her, aware she'd read his answer in his eyes.

Anger twisted inside him—anger at Lauren for making this so hard, anger at himself for failing to secure the vote.

'I won't stay here and watch them spend the country's money on trivia,' he growled. 'That is not an option. Neither would I leave my brother's son here to become a pawn in their power games.'

'But you can stay here—the answer's simple, you stupid man. You can marry a local woman—I've met dozens of wonderful Madani women—and you can rule as regent for Nim, and get to work on your dreams that have been put on hold for too long already.'

She paused, and the dread that had begun in his heart with her talk of his marriage to a local woman grew heavier.

'I will not leave Nim,' she continued, although she hadn't needed to put that into words to him, 'but he and I can live somewhere else, maybe close to the hospital, and I promise that there is no way I'd put your marriage or your reputation into any danger, neither would I do anything to hurt the woman you marry.'

'You don't love me?'

What else could he think when she spoke so calmly, so coldly?

'Of course I do. And I always will, but we have had our time together and I'll always have those memories.'

Another pause.

'Actually, I was thinking—those health outposts you want to set up along the nomadic tribes' regular route, the places where they always stop. You thought a nurse and perhaps an aide could operate them, doing regular health checks and vaccinations as the people come through. I'd be happy to do that. I already love the desert country. Nim and I can live out there. With the necessary books, I can homeschool him until he is old enough to go wherever older boys go to school.'

'You have it all worked out,' he said bitterly. 'You could walk away like that—as easy as you like—without a backward glance?'

'I didn't say it would be easy,' she snapped, 'but it would be a damn sight easier than living in town and seeing you, being near you, but not with you. Be reasonable, Malik, marrying someone else is what you have to do, so there's no point in getting all maudlin and lovesick about it. Your country needs you more than ever now there's been this split in the ruling parties.'

Malik just sat, trying to take in all she'd said, to process it so it made sense.

Which, of course, it did, even without much processing.

'You'd walk away from me?'

That was the hardest part to understand. What they'd had—to him at least—had been somehow more than love. It had been unique, sublime, so special words failed to do it justice.

'I wouldn't walk,' she said, so quietly he barely heard the words. 'I'd run!'

Then she bent her head and he knew she was crying.

He put his arms around her and pulled her onto his knees, and sat there, holding her, feeling her misery in his bones, feeling loss right through his body.

And for a long time there was silence, and the perfume of roses in the air.

And as she shifted, about to move, he tightened his hold as a new solution burned in his brain.

'I can have two wives,' he said. 'I suppose they'd insist the Madani one was the number one, but you could be my second wife—my real wife.'

She stood up now, looking down at him.

'As long as you treat both of them equally,' Lauren reminded him. 'Even I know that that is the law about multiple marriages. And quite apart from that, do you think I'd ruin another woman's life? She'd know herself a token bride, a political wife—how would that make her feel?'

Lauren wandered down the steps, and plucked a yellow rosebud from the nearest bush.

'My way is the best, Malik. You know that. Do it for Nim if not for yourself—so you have a wonderful, stable, happy country with healthy and educated people to pass on to him.'

And clinging to her last tattered remnants of self-control, she walked away from him, through the gardens to the front door, and hastily along the passages that led to her room.

There, at least, she could cry properly, although that wouldn't do much good.

But what she could do was look back on her memories of Malik and the special time they'd shared. She could wrap each one carefully then tuck it into a box deep down in her brain, to be taken out so far into the future that looking at them would bring pleasure rather than tears.

* * *

Work was the answer. Waking after a troubled sleep, Lauren showered and dressed for work, checked that Nim was up and ready for school, pretended to eat with him while he had breakfast, then asked Keema to call for a car to take her to work.

The young girl with rheumatic fever was her first stop on the ward. As she slowly recovered, more and more of her family were sneaking in, so the room now resembled one of the smaller nomad tents she'd seen in the desert.

Lauren checked the girl as the father spoke, a young family member, a lad of about twelve, now acting as interpreter.

'Your man, he is well?'

My man? she'd have liked to say, but if this man had obviously sussed out the tie between her and Malik it would demean what they had had for her to deny it.

'His problems are affairs of state,' she said quietly. 'He will do what is right.'

As the boy spoke the man gave a bow of his head. The simple gesture was eloquent with understanding, and gave Lauren a warm feeling of support.

She turned her attention back to the child, the lad translating rapidly so the conversation felt almost normal.

'Has someone told you that the tests show no damage to the heart, and because of that she will be able to go home soon?'

A different nod this time—all business.

'But she must rest until she feels ready to play again, and you will have to give her penicillin injections every four weeks—every twenty-eight days—for many years so she doesn't get it again.'

'Malik has told me this, and my sister, who trained as a nurse, will come back to live with us for a few months until I feel confident of doing the injections myself.'

Lauren smiled at him and waved her hands around the room where everyone, even the small children, was being very quiet.

Trying not to draw attention to their presence when the place looked like a fairground?

'Family is very special,' she said to the man. 'It is good your sister will help you for a while.'

'Family is everything,' the man said, and Lauren had to swallow hard and say a quick goodbye so she could escape before they saw her tears.

'You're stronger than this!' she told herself as she drew deep breaths in a cubicle in the bathroom. 'You *have* family, you have Nim. And Joe and Aunt Jane are as good as family—better even, considering all they have done for you.'

And now silently chastising herself for giving in to tears of self-pity, she returned to work, checked on the other children in the ward, made arrangements for a little boy with a broken leg who was returning home, spoke sternly to a mother who was feeding her recently diagnosed diabetic daughter with nougat, and generally fell into the routine that was work.

But as she talked with the aide who usually translated for her, and used some of the new words she was learning, she realised how much she'd grown to like this place—the hospital, the oasis, the country and its people.

For some reason, it had begun to feel like home, and although she knew, if she stayed, she'd be living in one of the small hospital accommodation units or a rented house, not a mansion with a rose garden bigger than a football field, she also knew that didn't matter. She could be happy here, she and Nim.

Malik would be too busy putting all his plans into practice to be at the hospital very much, and not seeing him would make things easier for her to bear.

Or maybe Malik would go ahead with his idea of the

health outposts—and she could live in the desert with Nim—that would be wonderful.

She shook her head.

No, it wouldn't—not for Nim. Not now she really thought about it. Even if he grew to love the desert as much as she did, he'd have no friends out there except when one of the nomadic tribes was camped there. But even those friends would move on.

She had to smile at how far her thoughts had wandered in the time it took for the aide to write out instructions for the storage of penicillin. Smile?

She'd actually smiled?

Well, she damn well wasn't going to *not* smile!

This was how it had to be, for these people she was just getting to know and admire, and for the country that was unique and needed to be protected.

And *she* was going to go about her work as if nothing had happened, no matter how hard that might be.

And at night, instead of dreaming of the man who'd brought her such joy, she'd plan the future—hers and Nim's.

She was in the staffroom, and as Malik walked in her head was already into planning mode.

Which was fortunate as it gave her a good defence against all her physical reactions to his presence and to the spasm of pain it caused in her heart.

'I'll need a house near his school and not too far from the hospital. I'm sure you'll do whatever has to be done about keeping Nim safe, and as long as it's not too expensive I can pay rent out of my hospital wages until I can organise to transfer money over here. And it would be good if we could move soon so there will be less chance of silly talk and scandal. And if we could keep Aneesha for Nim's language lessons and to help me learn as well, that would be good.

He stared at her as if she was an apparition, shook his

head, then walked away, whatever he'd come to say forgotten in her torrent of words.

But having said the words, and heard them in her own ears, the situation became far more real.

She could do this. Hide her broken heart and explain to Nim they were moving, learn how and where to shop for food, pack their things—could she take the trouser suits she'd been wearing for work, and maybe the lovely blue one…?

She sniffed hard, hoping to drain away the moisture collecting behind her eyes.

She *could* do this—she *would* do this…

Malik walked through the hospital in a daze. Knowing she was in the hospital, he'd hoped to find her and put his idea of them leaving to her once again—persuade her with love. Surely love would change her mind?

And he'd been met with a barrage of words that had stopped him in his tracks, and as he'd walked away, he'd realised she was deadly serious.

She would remain here in Madan, so he could rule for Nimr until he came of age.

Which left him where, exactly?

He tried to block out the answer to that question because it came in Lauren's voice.

He had to find a Madani bride!

How *could* he when he loved and wanted only Lauren?

What could he offer to another woman?

Certainly not love…

But Lauren was removing herself from the equation—and doing it deliberately because she was thinking of this woman—because without Lauren around he could least give his wife respect.

He groaned—aloud, it seemed, as several nurses passing by turned to stare at him.

Were they pretty?

Should he start to look?

He groaned again but kept it inside this time...

Nothing happened.

No new place of residence suddenly appeared, and Lauren had no idea where or how to start looking for something.

She could ask Keema for help, but it seemed disloyal to Malik to be discussing their personal lives, although everyone in the big house must know what was going on.

CHAPTER THIRTEEN

A FIRE IN a market on the edge of town brought in enough patients to keep all the staff busy for the next week, and although she didn't see him, Lauren knew Malik had been working every night because she saw his writing on the charts.

Well, she looked for it, and often looked just a little too long and touched it with her fingers when she did see it, as if somehow his written words could connect her to him again.

If you're going to stay here for ever you'd better get over this, she told herself one morning, but next morning looked again.

'Take some time off,' Graeme said to her, as she went off duty early the following week. 'The crisis is over—the children who need more care have been air-lifted out—and we're down to the ones who still need fluid replacement and their dressings changed.'

Lauren knew he was right. They were nearly back to normal, and she knew she was probably too exhausted to go on without a break.

She could look for somewhere new to live.

She needed sleep first, then she would look.

Her financial future wouldn't be a problem. She'd bought the duplex back home with money from her share of the sale of her parents' house but there was more. It was simply a matter of organising the sale of some shares and transferring some capital to a bank here.

At least Malik wouldn't have to pay her rent or, worse, buy her a house. How would his wife feel about that?

The word 'wife' still hurt, but she refused to not think about the unknown woman. It was for Nim, and the country he would one day rule, that she, Lauren, had made her decision, and she had every intention of sticking to it.

She was in the rose garden—could she plant roses in her new home, she wondered—when Keema found her. A Keema more excited than Lauren had ever seen her.

'Come, come, you must look and listen,' Keema said, taking Lauren's hand and practically dragging her into the house.

The television was on in the small salon, the screen showing a man in snowy white robes and white headdress on a platform in front of a large crowd.

'It is Malik,' Keema pointed out, although a glimpse of his shadowed face, and a flip of Lauren's heart had already told her that.

'He is speaking to the people—I will tell you his words,' Keema added, so Lauren stood and watched as Malik raised his hands and the excited crowd grew silent.

He began to speak, and while she didn't know the meaning of the words, Lauren heard a quiet determination in his voice.

'He talks of the new law,' Keema said. 'Talks of it being a bad law, for do we not live in a great wide world and should we not mix with the people of the whole world, whether for business, or pleasure—even marriage?'

Keema paused, and Lauren moved closer to the television, peering at the screen as if that would help her understand what was going on.

'He says the law tells him he must take a Madani bride, but is that the right thing to do, the good thing to do, if he loves another? He says he wants to marry and rule the country for his nephew, so Nimr will inherit a country that has good education—a university—and good care for sick people. I get the words muddled—'

Keema stopped, apologising for the delay. Listened again, then continued.

'He says that if it were not for the woman he loves, Nimr might not be alive, for the people who killed his father had been looking for him, although he was still only a tiny baby.'

Another pause, this time because the crowd had started shouting and Malik had to raise his hands to silence them again.

'He says the people who killed his brother also killed the family of the woman he loves—the brave woman who became a nomad to protect Nimr.'

Keema stopped again, turning to Lauren to ask, 'Did you do that?'

But Lauren was beyond speech. She had no idea where this was going, but tears were rolling down her cheeks as the man she loved with all her heart and soul spoke of his love for her...

'He says he wishes to do what is right for the country, but the new law says he cannot rule if he marries the woman he loves,' Keema whispered, tears running down her cheeks now.

On the television screen, Malik had stopped speaking for the noise from the crowd had grown so loud he could no longer be heard.

'What are they yelling?' Lauren asked, as the crowd waved their arms in the air and chanted a slogan or something else—the same words over and over again.

'They are crying out, "Marry her." They will not listen any more, they only cry *marry her, marry her, marry her*, all the time.'

And Lauren gave a rueful smile. Maybe if Malik became ruler and slowly brought in some form of democratic government, then the people would have some say in matters such as this—but for now, she knew, they had no power to alter the law passed by the council of elders.

But the words of the people warmed her heart and confirmed her decision to stay in this very different country—to stay and hopefully contribute to its future, to stay and make a difference if she could...

With Keema beside her, she was driven around the area—would it be called a suburb?—between Nim's school and the hospital. The houses were small, and of mud-brick construction, covered with earth-coloured plaster of some kind so they looked as if they'd been part of the landscape for thousands of years.

But inside many of them were new and modern, with two small bedrooms, kitchen and bathroom, living room and laundry, and, best of all, a large back garden, hidden from the front, but many of them already planted with fruit trees and roses.

'I live with my parents,' Keema explained, 'but I will ask my father about how you can buy one.'

'Could I rent one for a while?' Lauren asked, and Keema shook her head.

'I do not know that word but I will ask my father.'

And true to her word, she appeared the next afternoon with her father, a polite, middle-aged man in a business suit.

He bowed over Lauren's hand, and spoke to her in impeccable English.

'How can I help you?' he said.

'I need somewhere to live. Sheikh Abdul-Malik was kind enough to let me stay here while I found my feet, but now Nimr is settled in school and I am happy with my work at the hospital, I would like my own home.'

He bowed his head again, although she knew he must know there was more to her decision than she'd told him. After Malik's speech the entire country knew. Knew, also, that the law was the law.

She explained to her visitor that she must arrange money transfers from Australia before she would have the money to buy a property here but for now would like to rent one.

'And the Sheikh is not willing to make these arrangements for you.'

The implication of the words shocked Lauren. Keema's father was seeing her as a discarded mistress, believing it was Malik's duty to provide for her.

Well, in one way she was, she supposed, but...

How to explain?

'It is *my* decision to leave Abdul-Malik's house—mine, and mine alone. I wish to be independent, as I was back in Australia, but already I love your country and would be happy to remain working here. And I must think of Nimr, this is his heritage.'

And although inside she was a quivering mess, she managed to roll the 'r' on the end of Nim's official name quite well.

Then remembered Malik correcting her when first they'd met, and felt pain slice into her heart.

'You can lease our houses—this is something we have learned since the oil men came,' Keema's father was explaining. 'And more houses have been built for this purpose. But Keema tells me where you are looking—that is not a suitable place for you. There is an area where the ex-pats live—the houses there are better, more like Western houses.'

Which wasn't at all what Lauren wanted.

'Nimr is already at school here, and I would like to live close to his school. I believe he should grow up among his peers, the people he will one day rule—not among foreigners, no matter how convenient that might be.'

Keema's father bowed his head again.

'I shall find out what is available in the area where you wish to live,' he said, but Lauren had a feeling there was something behind his giving in without further argument.

She was proven correct when Malik arrived late that afternoon, a Malik she had never seen—coldly radiating anger.

'You have spoken to an outsider of our affairs,' he said, the words carrying the harshness of ground glass.

'Only Keema's father,' Lauren said. 'No one else. And it wasn't about you and I but about me finding somewhere to live.'

'And you did not think I would provide for you? Did you believe I would cast you both out of my home like so much unwanted rubbish?'

He stormed up and down the colonnade for a few minutes, perhaps so he wouldn't strangle her he was so angry.

Returned to stand in front of her.

'I have already had this house made over to you. It is your home—you will live here, not sneak off to some tiny house near the school.'

Maybe it was the 'sneak off' phrase that annoyed Lauren, but her temper was certainly rising when she said, 'Oh, for heaven's sake, Malik, have some sense. How's your wife going to feel if I'm still living in your home—living like a queen or, worse, a mistress? Will she believe you don't visit me, don't see me when you should be with her? I said I wouldn't harm your marriage in any way—and staying here would do that.'

The sudden flare of anger had burnt out quickly, and all Lauren felt was exhaustion.

So much had happened and she was tired and miserable. Heartbroken, in fact, but no way would she let Malik see that.

She turned away from him and wandered down into the garden, but even the abundant roses failed to give her solace.

Malik subsided into a chair and watched her in the garden, aware she was hurting as much as he was, regretting his anger, although he still felt it was justified.

Did she not really love him that she could just walk away like that?

Especially now things might change.

It was that he'd come to tell her.

He still could…

He stood up and followed her into the garden.

Stopped in front her, by a bush of pale lilac roses—his mother's favourite.

'I am sorry I was angry,' he said when she looked up at him, eyes blank of all emotion. 'I came to tell you the law might change—will change, I think. Or simply be deleted so the right to marry whomever one wishes will stand.'

He waited for a reaction, but none came.

'If that happens, we can marry,' he said, anxious now about her lack of response. 'I love you, Lauren, will you marry me?'

Her lips had moved, but as smiles went it barely fitted the description.

She walked away from him, pausing only to remove a dead rose here and there.

Then stopped and turned to him.

'The law hasn't changed yet,' she reminded him. 'And even if it does, would our marriage be the answer to the future? Won't the people who voted it in the first time be angered by the change—or more angered because they must already have been furious to have done that to you. Could it put Nim at risk?'

Malik shook his head.

She was right.

Changing the law changed nothing—except maybe to put Nimr back into danger.

He had information and supposition—some scraps of proof but nothing definite. Before they could move forward he had to prove his uncle's wife had been behind the so-called accident, and arrange for her to be detained or maybe exiled.

Which should have been his priority all along.

What an idiot he had been!

Here he was, running around trying to protect his own future when his brother's killers remained at large...

He bent and kissed her on the lips.

'Forget the house for the moment,' he said. 'Should you want one in another week, I will find one for you—where you want it, how you want it, I promise you.'

He kissed her again.

'But give me a week,' he said, then departed, because one more kiss and he'd have lifted her into his arms and carried her to bed.

Give him a week?

Two days into this allotted time—had she even agreed?—Lauren was no wiser as to what was going on. She was back at work so there was no time for house-hunting anyway, but of Malik there was no sign—not even a scrawled signature on a child's chart...

She worked, and at home continued her language lessons with Aneesha, going with her to the markets now and then to hear the language spoken all around her—steeping herself in it, and in the lives of the people.

She learned oranges were much prized, and that watermelons grew wild at some oases. She learned the names of many of the spices used in traditional dishes, and bought some beautifully embroidered, fine, silk shawls, even a few tunics that would go over the trousers she'd already been wearing.

But a shadow followed wherever she went, and as the days passed, it grew darker. To her way of thinking, Malik already knew who'd been behind the deaths. Was he concerned that his uncle might also have been involved?

His uncle was a blood relation, and the most important thing she'd learned in her time in Madan was the strength of family ties. For people who had begun as nomadic tribes, or were intermarried with such tribes, the family unit had always been their defence against outsiders—quite often in the past, it had been a physical defence.

So the last thing Malik would want to believe was that his uncle had been involved in his brother's death.

Lauren turned her attention back to work. She was in the nursery, in an isolation room, cuddling a baby with diphtheria.

'If Malik gets his way, your brothers and sisters will never get this horrible disease,' she told the baby as she rocked him to sleep in her arms.

She thought of all the good he could do for this country, and suddenly knew that staying here was probably *not* going to be an option. If *she* simply walked away— or flew—changed Nim's citizenship to Australian, which would surely cut him off from any position in Madan, then Malik would have no choice but to marry a local girl and get on with his life.

He would be ruler rather than regent, and his children would inherit and Nim would be safe.

It was so simple she didn't understand why she hadn't reached that decision earlier.

Because you love him...

The days passed slowly. The leopard cubs were too big now for Nim to safely play with them and he was back to wanting a rabbit or a dog.

He was happy at school, but he'd been happy back home. As she had been?

She shook her head, aware that 'kind of content' would be a truer description of her condition.

And I can be that again, she told herself, even with a pain that would lessen, but probably never leave her heart.

Again, it was Keema who hurried her into the small salon to see the local news.

'It is the wife of the sheikh's uncle,' she said. 'She is being banished from Madan.'

'And her husband?' Lauren asked.

Keema shrugged.

'They only talk of the woman, who must have done very bad things to be...you have a word, "exiled", I think?'

'Yes, exiled,' Lauren said, absentmindedly.

But that wasn't something she could talk about—not to Keema, or anyone at the hospital, although there too speculation was rife.

What could a woman have done to be exiled? people asked.

Had she cheated on her husband, which could, under local law, have had a much harsher penalty?

Lauren, aware of the answers, ignored the talk and gossip—and waited...

Malik came at dusk, playing with Nim in the garden, having dinner with the pair of them, talking of nothing much, his face so bland Lauren wanted to hit him for not telling her what was going on.

But with Nim in bed, they could wander into the garden, a place Lauren knew had become special to both of them.

'You saw the news?' he said, and she nodded, but when he said no more, she had to ask.

'She left alone. What of your uncle? Could he not have gone too? Will he not be heartbroken?'

Malik smiled at her.

'I tell you something and you think of someone else—someone who might be hurting.'

'I know about hurting,' she snapped, 'so of course I think of it. Was your uncle not part of it?'

'No! Not at all. In fact, he was horrified when she came to him a few days ago with a plan to hire someone to plant a bomb in a car to kill me, you and Nimr—to get rid of any opposition once and for all.'

'Horrified?'

Malik took her hands in his and drew her closer.

'He came straight to me, beside himself that his wife should think such a thing, let alone plan it, but the similarity to Tariq's death was what hurt him most, and he demanded to know if she'd planned that as well.'

'Did she admit it?'

Malik put his arms around her.

'Not right away, but when she saw his reaction she sneered at him, called him old and worthless, and demanded to know if he'd never realised how powerful it would make him to be rid of all his brother's children. He arrested her himself—called the palace guards and had her taken to the police station, but you're right, I couldn't let him see her face a public trial, so we chose this way.'

'We?' Lauren asked, needing to know the whole story for all she'd rather just be in his arms.

'My uncles and myself—the elders all agreed. To do more would embarrass my uncle and the country would look bad in the eyes of the world.'

'Oh, Malik,' Lauren whispered, and now she did move

into his arms, hugging him to her, the week that had seemed more like a year finally over.

It was a long time before they spoke again—apart from whispered promises of love.

But as they lay together in Lauren's bed, watching the dawn light creep slowly into the room, aware they had to part before Nim woke, Malik spoke of their future, of a wedding, of wanting to present the woman he loved to his people.

'We don't need to make a fuss,' Lauren said, but he kissed her opinion off her lips.

'I *want* to make a fuss!' he told her. 'I want the world—well, our part of it—to see the wonderful woman I am marrying. The woman who will help me achieve all my dreams for this country.'

He turned and took her face in his palms.

'I couldn't do it without you,' he said. 'I know that now. I knew it as soon as you sent me away and told me to marry a Madani woman. It was as if I'd lost my dreams as well as you. As if nothing mattered any more. I would happily have taken you and Nim back to Australia and lived there with you both, but you refused to let me run away. And you were right.'

He kissed her lips, a deep kiss of commitment, and gratitude and love, all wrapped up in the touch of lips to lips.

CHAPTER FOURTEEN

As PREPARATIONS FOR the wedding began, Lauren had to wonder what she was letting herself in for. To begin, Malik took her to the palace, an enormous, almost fantasy building, once again set in beautifully designed and kept gardens.

She was shown the state rooms that would be their new home, the huge salons where they would entertain both local and foreign dignitaries, then into a guarded and securely locked vault of some kind—as big as a bedroom—with golden treasures, precious stones, tiaras, necklaces, bracelets and rings set out along the shelves.

'Before we had oil—or knew we had oil—this was our bank, our insurance against bad times. For thousands of years the people have traded back and forth, and the ruling tribe has always kept enough of the treasures to add to this collection, so there would always be something to sell in order to provide food for the people, even in the leanest years.'

Lauren could only shake her head in disbelief at the beauty of the objects arrayed in front of her.

'A lot of these things were gifts—from one tribe to another—gifts exchanged. Other things were bought from travellers, either for their beauty or their value. But the personal things, they have been kept for the family, so you must choose a ring—it is tradition.'

'I couldn't choose one of these rings,' Lauren said, waving her hand at an array of dazzling rings in a glass case. 'I'd be uncomfortable wearing any of them.'

Malik smiled at her.

'Of course you would,' he said, 'but maybe this?'

He reached up high and pulled down a small box, opening it to show a beautifully cut sapphire, set in tiny diamonds.

'This is more you,' he said, and took her hand to slip the ring on her finger.

Where it fit perfectly!

'You planned this,' she said, grinning at him then checking the ring again to make sure it was real.

'I did,' he said, looking pleased with himself. 'I had Keema bring me the ring you sometimes wear that was your mother's to get the size and I knew this one was meant for you, so I had it sized and cleaned and there you are.'

'And Keema never said a word. She took me to look at houses, and still never said anything,' Lauren complained, but Malik just grinned at her, then kissed her, and held her left hand very tightly, as if he had to feel the stone on her finger to make it real.

The tour continued, and though Lauren looked around in wonder, there was a growing disquiet deep inside her.

Until finally she had to ask.

'Do we have to live here? Could you not be regent just as easily living where I am now?'

Malik shook his head.

'This is where the people expect me to be,' he said. 'This is where they wish to see me. Come!'

He led her down more corridors, back towards the front of the building, as far as she could make out, until they came to a huge room—more like a concert hall but open along the front and one side.

'This is where, on the first day of each month, people come to me with their problems. Ordinary people—school teachers, doctors, shopkeepers and street sweepers—anyone can come.'

'And you listen?' Lauren asked, thinking of the many times she'd visited her local councillor back at home for shade sails over the play equipment in their nearest park. He'd listened, agreed even, but as far as she knew there were still no shade sails…

'I listen, and do something to help if I can,' Malik assured her with a smile. 'I can't remember every request but I have some very efficient advisors who stand behind me and make notes of what needs to be done.'

'And can most things be done?' Lauren asked.

He nodded.

'Tariq and I, we often stood behind our father, listened to requests, then checked later if this system worked. We saw new wells sunk, and canals cleaned out in some of the suburbs, even once took a camel to a man who needed it as a dowry for his daughter so she could get married.'

Lauren laughed.

'Now, that I can believe you'd do.'

She thought about it for a while.

'Do women come? Or only men?'

'Mostly men, but I have been thinking—maybe we could begin a new tradition. The women could come and speak to you. We would have to find a suitable area—'

'In the garden,' Lauren said. 'They would be more relaxed there, and the children could run around.'

He reached out and hugged her.

'How could you have ever thought I could do this without you?' he demanded.

They wandered out into the gardens, finding an area shielded by hedges that would make a fine audience area.

'Thank you for this idea,' she said to Malik. 'Now I feel I can really help you follow your dreams, but right now I should go back to the house so I can organise more language lessons with Aneesha.'

He held her again, looking into her eyes, his own dancing with amusement.

'Am I not a good language teacher?' he teased.

And although she tried to remain cool and calm, she knew she was blushing.

'I already know the words you can teach me,' she said, and put her arms around him to hold him close, to rest her head against his chest and draw in the essence of the man she loved with all her heart.

But though he returned her hug, it was only momentary for there was far too much to be done.

'We need a date, and I must introduce you to the people as my future bride, and you must consult with Aunt Jane and Joe about when it will be convenient for them to come—and any friends of yours or theirs as well. We will send a plane. You will need a dress, no, two dresses, I think, one for the parade through town and the ceremony and one for the wedding feast with just friends and family and the council of elders and their wives—maybe a few hundred people, no?'

The words swirled around in Lauren's head like papers caught in a whirlwind.

So much for a small wedding!

They made their way back to the state apartments, and this time Lauren looked around the dark rooms ostentatiously decorated with treasures from the vault.

'May I change these rooms?' she asked, and Malik kissed her.

'Do whatever you like. My father's second wife deco-

rated them like this, but as well as the vault there are rooms
full of carpets and furnishings in the palace, and shops in
the city should you need something special. I must go to
work—work here, not at the hospital. I shall send someone
to bring Keema and Aneesha to you to help.'

'Thank you,' Lauren whispered as he kissed her goodbye.

Over the next days, with help from the two women, Lauren organised for all the treasures in the entire apartment
be returned to the vault, for surely they belonged to the
people, not to individuals.

'They should be put on display in the public rooms,' she
told the women, 'but we'll get on to that later.'

She looked around.

'The curtains have to go,' she said. 'Heavy gold dam-
ask is hardly the perfect choice for this climate. And all the
furniture, too. It is too heavy and ornate.'

Aneesha gave orders and strong men miraculously appeared to remove things, and while Aneesha stayed to
supervise, Keema and Lauren wandered through the palace, peeking into all the rooms, seeking things Lauren was
sure she'd recognise as right when she saw them.

It took a week, between shifts at the hospital, to get the
apartments emptied and painted in a sand colour, so pale it
looked white in some lights but golden in others.

And then the furniture Lauren had found in her hunt
around the palace began to appear. Low divans, piled high
with colourful cushions, a huge bed with a carved head-
board that looked as if it might have come from China mil-
lennia ago. Snow-white sheets and an ornately embroidered
silk coverlet Lauren had found hanging on a wall in a dark
corridor. A small table and two chairs were set beside the
window, dressed now with sheer cream curtains that bil-
lowed into the room in the wind.

With her two patient helpers, she then scoured the palace for carpets, knowing what she wanted for the bedroom—hand-woven silk on silk that was blissful beneath bare feet.

Her search took her to the back regions of the palace where, to her surprise, she found what could only be described as a village. Out beyond all the state apartments and housekeeping and catering sections of the palace she found the staff housing, with children running around kicking footballs and riding bicycles.

And although she was pleased, for Nim would surely find some friends among these children, it was an old woman that she sought. A weaver and expert on all traditional carpets and mats and camel bags who, she was told, knew every rug the palace owned.

Aneesha introduced them and translated, and the old woman, now retired, stood up and beckoned them to follow her.

She chatted to Aneesha as they walked through corridors unknown to Lauren and into a darkened room.

'She says these carpets are not for everyone,' Aneesha explained. 'She says the last woman could not have these carpets. She, the old woman, would not allow.'

Lights came on and Lauren stared in wonder at the beautiful carpets, piled on each other according to size, their dazzling colours a feast for the eyes.

'This one she made herself,' Aneesha said, and Lauren knelt to examine it, running her hands over the unbelievable softness, tracing the intricate patterns with her finger.

'May I have it?' she asked, aware just how special it was.

Aneesha translated and the woman beamed at her and nodded.

'She would be honoured,' Aneesha said, then followed the old woman to where she was turning back some carpets at the top of another pile, stopping at one in particu-

lar that sang with the colours of the desert in pale cream
and gold and red.

Lauren smiled and nodded, then asked Aneesha if the
woman would be willing to select all the carpets for her.

'Ask her if she will come with us to the apartments and
have a look, so she will know what they need.'

It took some time, but eventually the apartment was
finished, the muted colours of the furnishings Lauren had
chosen allowing the carpets to reveal their full magnificence, and turning the rooms into places of restful and el-
egant beauty.

'So, you will show me what you've done?' Malik asked
one evening when he called at the house for dinner with
her and Nim.

She shook her head.

'That's a surprise for you on our wedding night,' she told
him, then Nim was talking about his visit to the palace and
the children he'd met and, of course, the dogs.

'They are called saluki hounds and could I have one,
please?' he finished, and while Malik explained that they
were hunting dogs and he would have to look after it himself, see it always had plenty of fresh water, and feed it,
and take it for long walks for exercise, Lauren thought back
to the first day they'd had dinner together—in her small
kitchen back home.

Malik had spoken of these dogs then. How far they had
come…

CHAPTER FIFTEEN

THE QUESTION OF the wedding was still to be settled, Lauren baulking at the idea of hundreds of guests and two different dresses and the other things Malik had suggested.

'It is how things are done,' he said. 'And it is my opportunity to introduce you to the people.'

She smiled at him.

'I think I've already met a fair cross-section of the Madani people during the vaccinations or at the hospital. And after your impassioned plea for support, they all know about me. Can't we just be married quietly? Maybe later have receptions for guests?'

'So how would you like to be married?' Malik asked. They'd stolen a few quiet moments to themselves in his office at the hospital, Lauren about to go off duty and he abandoning affairs of state to give Graeme a break.

'Now I have options?' Lauren teased.

'Of course you have,' he said. 'There's the palace without the pomp and ceremony if you that's what you'd prefer. There's plenty of choice there. Or any one of the big hotels would be only too happy to make the arrangements.'

'And the rose garden?'

Malik smiled at the woman he loved.

'Really?'

She nodded.

'Unless you really need to have all that fuss you spoke of earlier—a wedding befitting your position—what I'd really like is something small and private in the garden, because, if you think about it, it's about us, not other people.'

And although he'd thought his heart was already full of love for this woman, he felt it swell with the emotion once again.

'I'm not the King, just the caretaker, and I can get married however I like. You're right, we'll leave the pomp and ceremony for Nimr when his turn comes. So the rose garden it will be. We'll just have Aunt Jane and Joe, and Nimr, of course, and anyone else you'd like, and my uncles, who are so contrite at what they did with the vote it will be like forgiveness to them.'

'Aunt Jane and Joe?' Lauren whispered, as if she'd doubted what she'd heard.

He smiled at her.

'Of course! I'll arrange to bring them over, and you might ask them if they'd like to stay a while and see Madan. Other friends, if you'd like. Maybe Peter Cross and his family if Susie is well enough to travel—it might be a little treat for them after all they've been through. I can send a plane so numbers don't matter.'

Lauren shook her head in disbelief. He'd only heard of Susie that one evening and yet he'd remembered her name. Although, being Malik, he'd probably talked to Peter and learned a lot more…

So! A wedding in the rose garden.

'It's like a dream,' she said quietly.

'But not one we have to wake up from, surely,' he said, getting up from the piles of paperwork on his desk and coming around to hold her for a few minutes.

They talked of dates again—ten days away—and times—early morning when the dew was still on the roses—and Malik was filled with a deep inner peace and happiness, two things that had been missing from his life since Tariq's death.

Later that day he went out to the house to have dinner with 'his family', taking with him a gift for Lauren.

'What is it?' she asked, holding the light, tissue-wrapped parcel.

'Open it and see,' Malik told her, and she did, Nim hovering by her side to see what was inside.

A long shawl in fine, palest pink silk, heavily embroidered with silver thread.

'Oh, it's beautiful,' she said, touching the delicate material with soft fingers.

'It was my mother's,' he told her. 'She wore it on her wedding day.'

Lauren set it down and hugged him hard, her throat too thick with emotion for speech.

But, she realised later, looking at the treasured gift, it solved the problem of what to wear for her wedding. Once she'd dismissed the idea of a massive royal wedding and two dresses to get through it, she had been through the seemingly endless racks of clothes in her dressing room, and although many of them were obviously for evening or formal occasions, she'd been unable to decide.

But seeing this, she pictured a rose-pink tunic that had pale pink and silver embroidery. With the scarf wrapped around her head instead of a veil, it would be perfect.

The days flew by. Joe, Aunt Jane and the Cross family arrived, much to Nim's delight, and while Nim took Joe, Peter and Susie out the back to introduce him to the animals and the vet who cared for them, Lauren and the two women went through the clothes in the dressing room.

For Nim there was a new *thobe*, or long white tunic, and

a new cap for his head, although Lauren had to put a stop
to him nagging Joe to also wear a 'dress'.

The day finally arrived, and Lauren and her 'family'
walked through the garden to the arch where white roses
grew from either side to fill the air with fragrance, their
spent petals forming a carpet beneath their feet.

And Malik fit right in, garbed in his snowy robe and
simple white square of headdress, held in place with a gold
cord.

Lauren felt her breath catch in her throat at the sight
of him, and for a moment she faltered. But she was close
enough to see the sudden concern in his eyes so she smiled
and kept walking, Nim by her side, Aunt Jane and Joe, the
Cross family, and Keema and Aneesha close behind.

They stood and made their vows, which were blessed
by an elder, then gathered in the small salon for a wedding
breakfast of surely unparalleled magnificence.

Roses decorated the centre of the table with bowls piled
high with fruit on either side. On the sideboard, an array of
dishes with mouth-watering aromas were being kept warm
over small heaters.

They ate and talked, and although Lauren would have
liked nothing more than to slip away with her new husband,
politeness insisted she stay.

But when they had eaten, coffee and sweet pastries were
served in the colonnade, looking out over the roses, and
she sat with Malik's uncles, assuring them she held no ill-
will against them.

Malik had wandered off with Joe, and Nim was telling
Aunt Jane about his school.

And there, in the garden, Lauren realised she'd found the
place that she belonged—Madan. She was already planning how to set up the health posts along the routes of the

nomadic tribes, a job Malik was only too happy for her to take over.

And Nim—she looked at his happy face as he explained about the leopards—had accepted this marriage with delight, assuring her when she'd stumbled through her explanation that he already knew people got married so they could sleep in the same bed…

She'd spoken to Aunt Jane and Joe, telling them she'd had solicitors draw up the papers to pass the ownership of her old home to Joe. Telling them also just how grateful she would always be to the two of them—taking care of her when she'd been broken by grief, coming to live with her to help with Nim—just being a family for her when she'd lost hers.

Telling them also that they were welcome to visit any time—that they would all love to see them…

Then Malik's voice broke into her rambling thoughts—Malik, her husband.

'And now,' he said, 'we come to the bride gift. It is customary in our family to give the bride a gift of money or jewellery that will provide for her should anything happen to me.'

He smiled at Lauren and added, 'Not that it will, my love, for how could I leave you?

'But my wife, who, as some of you already know, has decided views on many subjects, one of which, apparently, is not accepting such extravagant—as she calls them—gifts.' He paused to smile at his new bride. 'So I have been speaking to Joe, and with your permission, Lauren, I would like to give your bride gift to Joe for the organisation that he is now involved with—helping and training disabled defence force personnel, giving them a purpose in life and goals to aim for in the future, especially now the Invictus Games are growing into worldwide events.'

'Oh, Malik, that is a wonderful idea,' Lauren said, slip-

ping down into the garden to give Joe a hug, then turning
to hug Malik.

He held her close, just held her, but through the peace
that being in his arms always brought another thought sur-
faced.

'Can we go soon?' she whispered, and his body, so close
to hers, told her the answer.

And, as if by magic, the party dispersed. Aneesha had
arranged a tour of the country for the visitors and Nim—
trips to the lodge in the desert, and date farms, and oases,
camel rides, and nights under the stars.

But Lauren and Malik had a shorter journey—to the
apartment in the palace, where Malik shook his head in
wonder at the transformation.

'It's like being in the lodge, but in the city,' he murmured
as he took her in his arms, kissing her thoroughly before
they tried the big old bed for size and comfort.

'I love you so much, Mrs Madani,' he whispered.

'And I you!' she said, as a deep feeling of peace and
contentment settled into her heart—nestling up against
the brimming love…

* * * * *

LET'S TALK
Romance

For exclusive extracts, competitions
and special offers, find us online:

f facebook.com/millsandboon

⊙ @millsandboonuk

🐦 @millsandboon

Or get in touch on 0844 844 1351*

For all the latest titles coming soon,
visit millsandboon.co.uk/nextmonth

Want even more
ROMANCE?

Join our bookclub today!

'Mills & Boon books, the perfect way to escape for an hour or so.'

Miss W. Dyer

'Excellent service, promptly delivered and very good subscription choices.'

Miss A. Pearson

'You get fantastic special offers and the chance to get books before they hit the shops'

Mrs V. Hall

Visit millsandbook.co.uk/Bookclub and save on brand new books.

MILLS & BOON